# SINGAPORE WITH ABBY

by Captain George "Jake" Jacobssen USN (Ret.)

**DORRANCE**
PUBLISHING CO
EST. 1920
PITTSBURGH, PENNSYLVANIA 15238

Dorrance Publishing Co
585 Alpha Drive
Pittsburgh, PA 15238
Visit our website at *www.dorrancebookstore.com*

ISBN: 978-1-6853-7196-8
eISBN: 978-1-6853-7738-0

# Foreword

This novel was formed in my head that started from an actual experience when I was a very young Ensign, Naval Aviator, in the U.S. Navy on my first cruise aboard an aircraft carrier on a port visit to Singapore in 1950. The port visit was only for about six days but what occurred during that visit stuck in my mind over the years since and a story evolved that all began from that six-day visit. I hope you will find my adventures in this novel of some interest.

*To Silvia*
*from Jackson*
*old N'eval*
*and friend*

This novel is dedicated to that very lovely young
lady that I met in Singapore while on an aircraft
carrier visit in 1950.

*Jake Jacobsen*

# Chapters

# Chapter 1

# The Beginning

My name is Jake Janssen and I received my wings as a Naval Aviator and Commission as an Ensign in the U.S. Navy at Naval Auxiliary Cabiness Field located about ten miles west of Corpus Christi, Texas. My instructor's wife pinned my wings on to complete my two years in Naval Flight Training. I had been trained as a fighter pilot and was soon ordered to my first squadron, Fighter Squadron 192 stationed in Alameda, California.

Upon reporting, I was immediately involved in intensive training to become a fighter pilot. Following Fam we spent many hours and flights practicing fighter tactics, gunnery over the Pacific Ocean, and as an extension of the thrill of being in a fighter plane, much low level buzzing the hills, valleys, and beautiful mountains of California. A number of the new pilots, my friends, that is, Ensigns from flight training, had joined the Air Group and several to my squadron. Liberty in the Bay Area, mostly San Francisco, was very exciting for a bunch of wild ass young Ensigns. We were very large and noisy (we sang a lot of old Navy flying songs at the drop of hat) at every watering hole in the city. I remember one occasion when a buddy of mine and two great dates visited the night club "Mona's Candlelight." We guys knew it was a lesbian hangout so after we had settled in at the bar, my buddy and I slipped out to go to the john. When we returned to our dates, they insisted that we get the hell out of there fast, as they had been "approached" by several local ladies. We were BAD!

We were scheduled along with our Air Group to participate in a show the flag mission, over the major cities of the Far East. The cruise was to be a short one of only five months. The air shows that we conducted consisted of about sixty aircraft in flyovers. It was hairy, but we didn't lose anybody. We flew over Tokyo, Manila,

Saigon, Seoul, and Singapore. Great fun and quite an education in rendezvousing all those birds for the shows.

During a training flight from our carrier with about ten birds, before the flyover at Singapore, we were attacked by about six British Sea Furies. The Sea Fury was a good bird and we had about a ten-minute major simulated dog fight. Fun but lots of near miss collisions.

# Chapter 2

# Abby

We arrived in port at Singapore as scheduled and started enjoying the beauty of the old city and especially the famous Raffles Hotel. I remember sitting in the spacious bar of the Raddles drinking gin and tonic pretending we were old time British Colonels. We were still kids so this was quite an adventure. The second evening in port, the U.S. Naval Attaché threw a party/dance for us junior officers. It was a grand affair with free booze and the prettiest girls from the British community and European embassies. There was a sprinkling of Malaysian and Chinese young ladies, but most were white. We junior officers were dressed in our dress whites but no swords. There was a band that played rather subdued dance music with no jitterbug as we were used to. The young ladies were nicely dressed and friendly, mostly I think pleased to see so many eligible young men but also hoping for an invitation aboard our carrier for lunch.

The evening began as if we were back in a junior high dance as I remembered with the boys on one side and the girls on the other. I was a tad shy in those days as I had been reared in a boy's school, and now after 2+ years in this man's Navy, I was still not completely confident with young ladies. These young women were obviously the creme de la creme of the high society of Singapore. Very impressive for a young shy Ensign. Dancing started, and most guys were not as shy as I was and immediately started the action going by asking girls to dance. Not me! I had found the large open bar and was enjoying a tall, cool drink chatting with some of my old Ensign chums, when a beautiful red-haired young lady tapped me on my shoulder and asked if I would care to dance. She said her name was Abigail Scott but please call her Abby. She had a British accent and said she was a Scot (that explains the red hair). She apologized for being so bold as to have asked me to dance, but I told her that was just fine, as I was enjoying this girl. She told me she did not normally attend these type of functions, but a Mrs. Lawrence, who I found was the hostess for these type of gatherings whose job was to round up all the girls in town for these affairs. Later I met this charming lady and thanked her for her endeavors! Abby said she usually had too much studying to do to accept invitations to these affairs.

Abby explained that she was in pre-med training here in Singapore at the Royal British Hospital. She was pretty bold and had none of the shyness that I was af-flicted with. She said she had spotted me earlier (my goodness) and thought I was cute (good grief). She said she had her eye on me and hoped I would come ask her to dance, and when I didn't she said, "The heck with it," and would ask me. As we spent more together, I was very pleased that she was so bold. I'm a lousy dancer so after the first one I suggested that we step out onto the patio and chat over a toddy. She said she would like that, so we did. She told me she was born and raised in Sin-gapore and had only briefly visited Scotland once before World War II. Her dad was a doctor and her mother a nurse who had both been raised in Scotland and had met and married before the War in Singapore.

Abby was 13 when Singapore fell to the Japanese. I asked her what did her family do during the Japanese occupation of Singapore, but she sort of brushed that question away and changed the subject. Much more on that subject later.

We were obviously hitting it off pretty well together and sat out several dances on the patio as we were both enjoying one another's company. I asked her if she would be interested in visiting our carrier on the morrow, but she declined as she was studying for an important progresses exam the next day. I asked her to visit in the afternoon of the next day after her exam and she with a great smile said, "I would love to!" She then surprisingly asked me if I was hungry and I responded "always." She said she knew the best Chinese food restaurant and would love to take me there. Wow, I was making progress with this very attractive Limey! (I never called her that.) She said, "Let's go," and I quickly agreed. We said our thanks to Mrs. Lawrence. Abby asked if we might stop at her home or a minute and I of course agreed. She said her mom and dad were home and she would like me to meet them. I thought to myself I had never met any girl's folks so early before in a casual meeting. Off we went in her car, a tired old MGB that had seen better days. In Singapore we drove on the wrong side of the street (at least to me as an American). Abby must have known all the cops in town as she had a very hard foot on the gas pedal. Scared me but I was getting pretty interested in this redhead so didn't say a word!

Abby's folks were very nice and curious as to what their daughter had brought in. I was hopefully pretty presentable in my whites and burr haircut. We only spent a few minutes with Dr. and Mrs. Scott, and Abby told them she was taking me to Chang's for dinner. The Scotts were obviously familiar with Chang's and said, "Have a good time and say hello to Chang." Mrs. Scott as a caring mother reminded Abby that she had a big exam coming up and not to stay out too late.

Off we went for another white-knuckle drive to the restaurant. Abby certainly knew her way around town and found the last parking space at Chang's. We entered, and the tallest, heaviest Chinese man I had ever seen enveloped Abby in a big bear hug. He scolded her for not having visited for a while. Abby untangled herself from this giant and obvious dear friend and scolded him right back for crushing her in his greeting. Abby introduced me to Chang and she said she owed her life to this colorful gent. She provided no details as to that comment, but it certainly caught my interest. I thought that I'd query her later about that remark. Chang seated us, and without our ordering anything or even seeing a menu, they started to bring food. It was overwhelming but the best Chinese food that I had ever eaten. Chang supervised our serving though he had a full restaurant of customers. It was very clear to me that Abby and Chang had a special relationship and I was very curious how that had occurred. I ate until I was about ready to pop, and I noticed that Abby was keeping up with me. I later learned that Abby always ate like a Marine and never seemed to put any weight on. I found that she ran about five miles every morning before breakfast. That explained how she maintained a great figure! That was something I noticed from the get go and realized she was very nice to look at. I noticed when we got into her car for our death defying trips that she wasn't concerned that her dress would ride up showing me her passenger some very attractive legs. But I digress! It was a very delightful dinner as Chang hovered over Abby as though she was his personal property. It was interesting to watch this large, hulking Chinese guy paying so much attention to this lovely Scottish girl. Interesting. As Abby's escort Chang seemed to tolerate me and gave the impression that if I were to put a hand on Abby uninvited I might find myself broken in two and thrown out on my ear! I said to myself I had to find out how a beautiful young Scottish girl had ever become so obviously a tender target of this gent's affection!

I got Abby home pretty early as her mom had suggested. We made a date to meet on the pier that was accommodating our liberty parties at 2 p.m. the next day for our tour of my carrier. This late time would preclude a lunch aboard, but I could show her the working of an American aircraft carrier.

I showed her the catapults and arresting gear and explained how an aircraft landed and caught a wire for an arrested landing. We made a tour of the island and I showed her the bridge. She seemed interested and asked lots of questions, most of which I could answer. I took her to our ready room and introduced her to several of my squadron buddies who were lounging around before going ashore on liberty. It was a fun tour and she asked me if I would like to join her family for dinner that evening. I of course said yes, and she said she would pick me up on the pier at 6 p.m. I escorted her ashore and helped her into her car and off she went.

She arrived on time, and after a hairy ride to her home, we settled in with her mom and dad. I met a new member of the family who was also loved and cherished as was Abby. He was Richard and was 14. Nice kid in his sophomore year in high school, though they called it something else. I found that Dr. Scott was a reserve surgeon with the British forces there in Singapore in addition to his daily medical chores in private practice. Mrs. Scott had retired as his nurse and was now a home body and lady of leisure, if you call golf, tennis, and children's hospital volunteering leisure. Abby told me she had another year to go as a medical student and then off to the U.K or the U.S. for her residency in pediatrics. Her plan was then to return to Singapore and work with the many children in poverty in the city and the surrounding villages.

I was still curious as to what this family did during the Japanese occupation of Singapore. You'll remember that Singapore, though heavily manned by the British Army, had fallen quite quickly as the Japanese forces moved down the Malaysian peninsula attacking Singapore from the rear. I recall reading something about the British big guns were not available to point to the "rear" of Singapore from where the Japanese attacked but were pointed seaward to the south. Dr. Scott, a Reserve Colonel, said he had been interred in a Japanese prisoner of war camp but said nothing more.

The dinner was delightful with much friendly and affectionate banter between the family members. They asked me a number of questions about the U.S. though they were all pretty well informed about the States as they had visited California after the war checking on Stanford University as a potential residency location for Abby when she finished medical school.

After dinner, Abby showed me to her room. It didn't seem strange to her folks, but it did to me. No problem. I asked her flat out about what happened to her and the rest of the family during the occupation. She said that she and her brother Henry and her mom had been put into a British dependents prison camp. She was 13 when she entered the camp and was a skinny kid with a great deal of red hair. I didn't get many details until after we were better acquainted except the Japanese guards were very cruel and food was very scarce. There was little medicine, food, and clean water. She and her brother were allowed to remain with their mother in the corner of a grass-roofed hut that leaked badly when it rained. There were about 200 women and kids in the camp. There was a sprinkling of domestics who had been interred with their employers. There were little bathroom facilities so they dug ditches to do their business. There were some older women and pregnant women in the camp who suffered badly. I was told that she preferred to have her color called auburn not red! She didn't like to be called a redhead. Live and learn. That evening conversation opened a world of information for which I was very curious, but Abby was a tad reluctant to talk about her imprisonment in detail until we become better acquainted. I must admit I found this "auburn" headed girl to be fascinating and was extremely interested in finding out much more about her Japanese experience!

I asked her if we might have a picnic the next day. Wow, was that that a great idea on my part. She said she loved picnicking and knew just the right spot on the shoreline which was very private and beautiful with a magnificent view. She suggested that we meet on the carrier pier and she would have a picnic basket all pre-pared for our outing. I was a pretty smart guy to suggest a picnic as it would give us privacy and perhaps give me the opportunity to learn more about her POW years! I have to admit that it might also give me an opportunity to kiss those beautiful lips that I had been eyeing since I first met her. In the few girls I had dated at home, none had grabbed my attention as did this beautiful Scot!

# Chapter 3

# The Fence

We rendezvoused as planned on the pier and she had packed a picnic basket loaded that could have easily fed the Russian Army.

We drove (hold on to your hat) to a very nice private beach on Manna Bay with a view of the Singapore Strait. I brought up the Japanese camp she had been in with her mom and Richard with questions about how long were they in the camp. How were they finally released? Who released them? What kind of shape were they in physically? She for the first time seemed ready to talk about her camp time. When Singapore fell to the Japanese, all military personnel, including her dad, had been rounded up and were separated from their families and were put into temporary enclosures while their more permanent POW camps were built. They were very roughly treated as Japanese considered them very cowardly and weak as Singapore had fallen so quickly under the Japanese assault. Many were initially killed if they offered any resistance. Their home was occupied by Japanese officers and was used as a clubhouse and brothel. Abby and her mom and Richard were immediately separated along with all British citizens from their men folks and were put into their own camps.

Three months after Abby and family entered their camp, Richard, in his wandering around the camp, found a shallow spot under a section of fence that was close to his family's hut. He showed it to his mom and Abby, and they both told him not to mention it to anyone. Abby thought about it for a long time and wondered if she with her skinny frame might be able to slide under the wire to freedom! She realized that the shallow spot would have to be made a little deeper and a tad wider for her to slip under the fence. She and Richard went on the lookout for some sort of tool that would assist them in making the hole larger. Several of the guards had started gardens, and Abby spotted a hand trowel that was left out at night and she set her plan to steal it. Theft was not something she had ever been good at, but now with the need for freedom, theft became an obsession with her. On the next wet and rainy night, she slipped out of her hut and did the deed and came home richer by one garden trawl.

She told Richard that she had a tool to enlarge the crawlspace under the fence but was afraid that if they were caught digging they would be severely punished, perhaps even killed. Richard asked her if she was to get out would she come back. Abby told him he was nuts; if she ever got out it would be katy bar the door. She would be gone. Richard wanted to know if she was planning to take him with her. She said of course. Richard said he was reluctant to leave their mother. Abby agreed that that would be a big consideration for them if they ever decided to escape. Their mother solidified their plan when she became very ill and weak. Abby decided that she needed more food and medicine so she decided to escape but try to find food and medicine for her mother so she planned to return! She started her plan by first recording the times of the guards who walked the perimeter of the camp. They had fallen into a routine so Abby detected a 25-minute gap between the times they came past the potential escape hole. There were searchlights but they were seldom used by the guards. Abby developed a plan whereby she and Richard would dig open the escape hole and then she would wiggle through the opening and be on the outside and Richard would replace the dirt so the escape hole would not show. They practiced this procedure during the 25-minute respite several times and finally decided that their mom's condition was worsening so they planned to get Abby out to hunt for food and medicine. They told their mother about their plan, but she forbid them to try as she believed that if were caught they would be put to death. As her condition worsened, the kids decided to disobey her and carry out their plan.

On the first moonless night, they planned to carry out their plan. They didn't have to wait long for a clear, dark night. They waited after the guard passed and knew they had 25 minutes before he would return. With their trowel, Richard and Abby cleared enough of the soil under the fence for her to creep under it. Once outside, she started walking toward some lights not sure where she was or where she was going. Meanwhile Richard returned the earth to the hole they had dug and went back to his hut to await Abby's return.

Abby was concerned that she had not planned on where to go to obtain help for her mother. She didn't have to wait long as she was grabbed by two men, one a tall large Chinese and the other a small Malaysian associate of the big guy. They didn't hurt her but were curious as what a white girl was doing wandering around apparently lost in the middle of the night. Abby told them where she had come from and with that they marched her several miles into the jungle to meet their leader. When they arrived at the leader's encampment, they were surprised to see so many men there. It seems that they were guerillas fighting and harassing the Japanese while hiding in the jungle. The Japanese seldom came into the jungle to find them as they were entirely elusive and it was very hazardous for the Japanese searchers.

The leader was Chinese named Dr. Andrew Lee who was quite well known in peacetime Singapore as an educated and active pediatrician working with the poor while managing a large parcel of land left to him by his father. Abby had met him through her father and while she was in med school at the Royal British Hospital. She had never spoken to him but was aware of his work with children.

When she told Dr. Lee her name was Abigale Scott, he asked if her father was Dr. Scott who Dr. Lee knew very well. She of course acknowledged her identification. Dr. Lee was very curious as to what she was doing wandering around in the dark by herself. She explained that she had temporarily escaped from her dependents prison camp and she was seeking aid for her mother. She was dirty and tired and frightened by what had occurred this night and cried when Dr. Lee told her he would help her as best he could. He said he would give her food but no medicine as he did not know what was ailing Mrs. Scott. He had his men rig a backpack for Abby and gave fruit and vegetables to take for her mother. He said he would provide an escort for her back to her camp. He directed the large Chinese man who had captured her to be her escort home. His name was Chang!

Abby told me that she thanked Dr. Lee and told him she could come out from her camp any dark night. He said, "Fine, but you need help in coming to me after you have escaped from the camp." He said, "We would need some kind of signal when you are coming out so I can have someone meet you." Abby said that her mother and she used a clothesline behind their hut and so whenever she was going to come out they would hang a red shirt on the clothes line. Dr. Lee agreed and said they would watch for the signal, and if she came out someone would meet her and they would escort her to Dr. Lee's camp.

When Abby returned to her camp, she had arranged a signal with Richard to dig open the area under the fence for her return. They would then refill the hole with the dirt. This all sounded pretty simple and routine when Abby told me this story, but their timing and signals had to be precise and timely with an eye out for the rotating guard during each sojourn. Abby discussed this adventure as though it was an everyday occurrence. It was of course not that, and the fact that it was years ago when she was teenager seems to have mellowed the adventure in her mind. I was flattered that she felt comfortable enough with me to tell me the story of her adventurous life. There's more.

When she gave the food to her mother, there was hell to pay as her mom was extremely concerned with the safety of Abby and with Richard for his part. She told them she would rather die of starvation than lose either one of them to their captors. She started eating the food that Abby had brought and in a very few days began to gain strength and energy. Remember she was a nurse and was frequently called upon to help other prisoners with their health issues. She was particularly called to help the older women and the pregnant ones. With her renewed strength, Abby pled with her mother to let her make another trip outside to get food and medicine for the needy. Her mother realized that some of the elder women might not make it without additional food from Abby's trips. After much soul searching, she agreed to allow Abby to make another trip outside for food. They hung the red shirt on the clothesline, and on the next black night Abby and Richard did their thing and Abby was met with her new friend, Chang, outside the fence. Dr. Lee was pleased that Abby had come again and she realized that they now had a conduit to get help into this dependents camp to help save lives. With this beginning, Abby, with her mother's new blessing, continued her trips over a period of the next three years, never being caught. The trips for food and meds later were estimated to have saved the lives of over 100 women and small children. Abby told me that after the war her count of trips outside of the fence totaled 65.

My respect for this girl soared as I heard her story. She came out of the war unscathed with the realization that her bravery had saved many lives and had cemented strong friendships with Dr. Lee and his man, Chang! Abby said that she was fortunate enough during her brief visits with Dr. Lee to discuss her future and her desire to become a doctor and work with the poor and underprivileged children of Singapore.

I later found that she had failed to mention that after the war, King George the VI invited Abby and her parents to London for her to be awarded "The George Cross" for bravery for her heroic efforts to save the lives of many during the Japanese occupation of Singapore. The Cross also brought her the title of Lady as part of her name. So now here I was being dazzled by a beautiful auburn-haired Lady Abigail Scott! Not so shabby!

We had three more days to be together before our carrier sailed away. I'm afraid I took her away from her studies as I monopolized her time with dinners, picnics, and movies together. Abby was to graduate from med school in six months and then was hoping and planning to go here once accepted to do her residency in pediatrics. It became pretty obvious they Abby was attracted to me as I was to her. We discussed how we could continue our budding romance with me leaving and being in the Navy and she pursing her medical training. I started to have ideas about resigning my commission and joining Abby in her life wherever. I discussed this idea with her and she said if we could continue our friendship it might just be that we would fall in love and marry. She said that she was beginning also to have those types of feeling already and said she would follow me wherever I wanted to take her. I told her that the Navy owed me two more years of college from my original contract. Perhaps I could be accepted to Stanford where I had desired and wanted to go for those two years, and if Abby applied there we would be together for a couple of years. She liked the idea so now we had the problem of both being accepted at Stanford. I told her I was falling in love with her and if we both ended up at Stanford we ought to get married first or we would probably end up living in sin, which would drive both of our parents up the wall. These discussions went on for the next couple of days as we continued to fall in love and tried to figure out how we could best be together. If I were to resign my commission it would take a while and my ship was not scheduled back to Singapore as far as I knew. I did know that we were scheduled for Hong Kong for an eight-day visit in a couple of months. Abby said that she and family had been going to Hong Kong once a year since the war for shopping and vacation and perhaps she could convince her folks to do it this year at the same time as my ship's visit there! Problem solved at least for a while, and it would give us more opportunity to discuss our future.

You can only imagine Abby's folks' response to her request to arrange their annual trip to Hong Kong to coincide with my ship's visit there. I think they were suspicious that they may be losing their daughter to a sailor from the U.S. They seemed to like me as I liked them, but I think they thought that Abby would be presently leaving Singapore to be with me in the U.S. The suspicions were well founded as I hadn't thought about settling down in Singapore but had always assumed I would spend my life in the U.S. Dr. Lee got his oar in by inviting Abby and me to dinner at his home. He lived very well with a beautiful and gracious Chinese wife and a house full of servants. His father had been very successful as a businessman in the area. He had been awarded 250 hectares of land in Queenstown Area by the Crown for work he had done for the British Government during WWI. He was one of the largest landowners in Singapore with the exception of the city government. Dr. Lee did not mince any words as he allowed that he had most fervently hoped and expected that Abby would one day take over his pediatric practice and follow his actions as he had devoted most of his services for the poor and underprivileged children of Singapore. It was no surprise to Abby, but though I had gotten wind of his desires, this sealed his desires in concrete. Meanwhile back at the ranch, Abby's folks decided to agree to Abby's request to spend their Hong Kong vacation with me in that port!

The arrival of our ship in Hong Kong was of course was joyful. I had not sent my papers into resign my commission as the North Koreans had crossed into South Korea and I did not believe my request would be approved. Everyone was saying that General McArthur would hold the line and the North Korean excursion would not last long. Abby had requested admission to Stanford to pursue her residency. Dr. Lee had used his influence with Stanford leadership, and it appeared as though her application was a lock! Dr. Scott had reserved a suite in the Hilton in Hong Kong, and I even had a couch in the suite so I did not need to return to my ship every night. It became very obvious that Abby and I had fallen deeply in love during this port visit. Her parents were pleased but on several occasions asked me what were my intentions if I was able to leave the Navy. I'm afraid my answers were a tad waffled as I wasn't sure myself.

The Chinese made my decisions for me as 300,000 screaming Chinese joined the fun to my shipmates in our squadron, I did not believe it was right for me to leave the Navy in the middle of a lousy war! Fast forward, Abby was very unhappy with my decision not to leave the Navy as she was naturally accepted at Stanford when they became aware of her dynamic war record and awards by the crown. She was accepted for a two-year residency, and I remained in the squadron for a full seven months' tour, flying from my carrier during the Korean War. As you can imagine, we filled the coffers of post office mail and talking tapes during those seven months! As our tour was nearing an end, I submitted my resignation and at the same time applied to Stanford for the last two years of my original Navy contract.

To make a long story short and end this part of my tale on a happy note, my resignation from the Navy was accepted as was my application for my last two years of college at Stanford. Abby met my ship's return to the States and it was a joyous reunion. The first thing on our agenda was to get married. Mrs. Scott was planning to come to California and help with the wedding planning. It happened with Dr. Scott giving Abby away and my folks there with my mom's tears setting our future life in concrete.

We found a small one-bedroom apartment in the home of a lovely older widow who we surmised rented out the apartment to have some company during her old age. Her name was Ida Johnson and insisted everyone call her Aunt Ida. She was a wonderful addition to our twosome as she fell in love with Abby as did most people. We dined with her at least once a month and we had her into our little place on all holidays as her family all had gone to Heaven. It was a wonderful relationship for us and for her!

Now economics! I was in college on a Navy contract that paid my tuition, books, and fees plus a whopping $75.00 a month. I had saved up $3,000 during my time in the Navy, but this was hardly going to sustain us for long. Abby had a year to go in her training, and I was faced with two years of school. Abby's expenses were well taken care by her folks plus she had a small allowance.

In *The Stanford Review*, a local newspaper, I spotted a tiny advertisement for former military pilots to work as crop dusters in the Santa Clara Valley. The location was close enough to school that the old jalopy that Dr. and Mrs. Scott had given us as a wedding present could get me to and from the dusting home site near Santa Clara. Again I had fallen into it; the owners of Santa Clara Dusting were a delightful young couple with two small kids that had bought the dusting business from a retiring older couple. Jim and Sara Maple were the owners. Jim was former Air Force and he had also flown in Korea. They were pretty new to the dusting business but had inherited a clientele that had been loyal customers of the old owners and were ready to continue their relationship with the new owners. Jim had three other pilots on the roster, an interesting mix of former military guys and old fud civilian pilots. It was a heck of an interesting group, but it was a job and they paid pretty well for a job that few would or could do. Abby wasn't very excited about me taking this flying job as she was concerned that I might get badly hurt if I wasn't lucky. I was lucky and never crashed but did have an engine failure one morning but was able to set the bird down in a level field. Most of our dusting was in the morning at first light to avoid the winds that came up later in the day. I was able to arrange my classes to the afternoons so it worked out and I was able to bring in enough cash for us to live pretty comfortably. Dusting is exciting! It's legal buzzing but at low speeds. You had an associate on the ground with a large flag who marked the row of the crops that you were dusting. At the end of a row, you would do a wifferdill (sort of a low altitude wing-over). It was a sort of a quick 180-degree turn to get on the next row. It frankly didn't take a lot of brains but did require some pretty good skill in seat of the pants flying. I was paid $50 bucks for a single regular field, a little more for a very large field, and could normally do two fields in a morning. I flew many weekends that increased the $50 pay to $65 bucks. In a week of decent weather and no winds to worry about, I could earn about $700. I'd never get rich, but it did reinforce our lifestyle.

I had switched to Political Science in my studies, concentrating on Russian and Soviet politics and happenings. My professors were mostly old Russian gents who had been able to get out of Russia before Stalin's cruelties. Abby was becoming experienced in her work with children. Stanford had a relatively large hospital with a large section devoted to working with kids. Abby was thriving in her work, and I was studying when I wasn't flying and driving back and forth to my dusting job. We were able to find time for making love, many times at the drop of a hat. She thankfully enjoyed loving as much as I did.

Many times we discussed our future. She knew that wherever we ended up she wanted to start her practice as a pediatric surgeon and child caregiver. I frankly didn't know what I wanted to do. I did not want to teach and I wasn't preparing myself for many other enterprises. There wasn't much doubt in my mind that she wanted to return to Singapore and work with kids as Dr. Lee had offered. Her mom and dad of course fully endorsed that idea. We had the problem that Abby was going to finish her training a year before I was finished with my two years of study. She could perhaps return to Singapore for that year, but as far as I was concerned, it was out of the question. I loved this lady so much I wasn't about to have another long separation. That problem soon found a solution as Abby was asked to take a position in the hospital to continue her work with her kids. Whew, thank the Lord for that solution to our problem!

Dr. and Mrs. Scott visited with us one summer while we were in California. I now was addressing them as Mike and Eleanor, and me as Jake, though I suspect he would have preferred me to be more formal with Michael. Sorry, he was stuck with a smartass fighter pilot who was as American as you can get! I found out later that Eleanor and Abby had had a long conversation as to what our plans were for children, ours not Abby's patients. Naturally, Abby and I had talked about kids but were taking the right precautions to wait until we were finished, me that is, with our studies and were somewhat settled into our next adventure (where?) like work.

Mike said he had some good connections in Singapore and was sure he could find some work for me if we returned. It was a serious dilemma for me as I knew that returning to Singapore was in Abby's thoughts, and the return there with no promise of employment was a tad scary for me. Nevertheless, our plans started to form to return, if only to satisfy Abby's most fervent desire to help the kids of Singapore! I was resolved that I could find something to do, what I had no idea.

# Chapter 4

## Return to Singapore

We booked our return to Singapore with Dr. Lee who had been visiting California on business and had stopped by Stanford to visit with old friends and Abby and I, and attend my graduation. He was returning as we were so we shared a three-seat center isle on the big bird and he and I had a conversation that would change my life forever!

He offered me a job with a salary I couldn't turn down. He wanted an assistant who was white, as all of his senior employees were either Chinese or Malaysian and he needed someone who could better interface with his business partners in the U.S., Britain, and Europe.

He had plans for expansion of his business to worldwide customers. I'm getting ahead of myself. Dr. Lee's business had been inherited from his father; his land was mostly involved in rubber production. He owned a lot of land that he believed with the right folks he could greatly increase his business. He thought that I might be the idea man he needed to help with his expansion. I read between the lines and realized that if he could convince me to stay in Singapore it would keep Abby there as I am sure that was his primary thought. I agreed and planned that in spite of my total lack of knowledge of what he had in mind, I might surprise him and myself and more than earn my keep.

He told me about his senior employees' resident campus and stated that a modest house with a car (an old one) and servants awaited us. Died and gone to Heaven I believe they called it! Abby was excited about the opportunity that Dr. Lee was offering as she had faith in me that I could more than do whatever he expected of me. I wasn't stupid and realized that all of these opportunities were coming my way because of the love and respect that Dr. Lee had for Abby. Me too! I was bound and determined that Dr. Lee would someday look upon me as a heck of a bonus he was getting with Abby.

With our return to Singapore, we moved in with Mike, Eleanor, and Richard temporarily. Richard, like his sister, had enrolled in medical school there in Singapore. He said he wasn't going to take care of poor kids but to concentrate on rich folks and become wealthy himself. Stand by that will change!

Now to work. Abby was readily accepted in the Royal British Hospital as many there knew her and were aware of her skills as a budding pediatric doctor. I reported to my first day of work with Lee Industries. Dr. Lee introduced me as his assistant to his senior staff of employees. I found that I was the only white face in the group. I recognized that there was not a lot of hooting and shouting to have this new pale face in their organization. I realized it was only my introduction and it would take some time and a major effort on my part to be accepted by this group. Dr. Lee offered to take me on a tour of his land, which I was most anxious to see. Dr. Lee showed me a small office that was next door to his large, well-decorated office. I told him my concern as being the only non-Asian on his senior staff. He said I was not to worry as the senior gentlemen would get used to me. He drove in an old jeep, which he drove around and through his large rubber plantation and down a slight hill to his mining operation where ore was extracted and hauled to the separation plant where tin was extracted. The narrow roads that we traveled on were rough and barely passable. I suggested that perhaps he need horses to travel his property. He listened but did not comment. He told me that I could travel anywhere on the company's property but to be sure to have a gun bearer with me as he still had a few tigers on the property! Holy Moses!

He had a secretary take me to our assigned furnished house as promised. There was an old Buick in the garage, and a man and a woman, both Malaysian, were there in the house as our servants. The secretary Lisa said the house was ready for my wife and me to move into whenever we were ready. That night I told Abby about my first day and that the house that was ready for us. She asked if it would be okay to move in after work. I said I had been told anytime. After work the next day, we moved in. We had little in the way of furniture with a few items from Abby's folks' house. The servants were named Petung and Uni. Abby, who spoke the local dialects immediately began a conversation with them. They were married to one another and had been working as domestics for several years. They seemed happy to have us move in and give them something to do. Uni was also the driver of the Buick and was raring to go to show off his driving talents. Petung was the cook and said she needed to go to the market soon to buy groceries. Abby said she would give her a list, which they would make out together, and she could go to the market the next day. So we began our life with me as an employee of Lee Industries as assistant to the president. On my second day of work, I visited each of the five senior staff in order to become acquainted, and as I had done in my Navy jobs, indicated that I had very little knowledge as to the working of Lee Industries and needed much help in doing my job. Always worked in the Navy and it brought folks around to help me get settled in my new job. I soon realized it was going to take more than a hat in the hand attempt to be accepted! I think maybe I was a threat to their usual routine in running the company. I took the jeep with an armed guy riding shotgun and wandered over the entire Lee Industries property. The most surprising observation was a "hole" in the center of the land that smelled of gas and oil.

# Chapter 5

## Lee Industries

My first impression was that Dr. Lee had a heck of a lot of land going to waste. It needed clearing in most areas, but then when cleared it would be ripe for all sorts of enterprises. It appeared to me that for some reason Dr. Lee had neglected to prepare his land for expansion. I came to realize that his failure to utilize the land in a profitable manner was his dedication to the poor and underprivileged kids of Singapore. He spent most of his day in the hospital working with the children and doing miraculous work in saving lives and restoring children to full health. I began to realize that he saw in me the hopeful way to utilize his land as he just didn't have time to do it!

I thought that there was plenty of labor available to help clear the land and establish money making projects. There was still much poverty and property remaining in Singapore from the Japanese time. Work was what was needed, and I could envision all sorts of labor that would be needed to satisfy my ideas. I should note that I had made up a list of potential projects to be established on Dr. Lee's land. I of course would need his approval and money to get these projects off the ground. Here is my list of projects:

- Clear the land as needed for the projects
- Check with the local economy for feasibility to sustain the projects
- Install livestock: cattle, pigs, chicken.
- Investigate the potential of the gas and oil leak
- Sugar cane and sugar mill
- Cultured pearls (Mickie Moto style)
- Transportation to get the products to market

I am the first one to admit that this list was very ambitious and would involve much labor and money to accomplish. I took the list to Dr. Lee, and happily he didn't throw me out of his office. He liked the list but suggested we proceed slowly and intelligently and not to run off half crazy.

He was somewhat enthusiastic about my plan. Where to start? I needed intelligent advice as to whether the economy of Singapore was ripe for my ideas and could the project be profitable. I figured I needed advice so I went to the American Embassy and asked for the economy guys. I was ushered into a large office with a big gent present. His name was Charles Greene. I told him what I was there for and told him I needed professional advice. The guy was a good find and had been in Singapore since the war. He knew Singapore's progress since the war and her needs for the future. He liked my plan and said the livestock beginning would be well received if the prices were maintained at a reasonable level. He said the people of Singapore had skimped on meat due to its availability and he said there was a ready market for meat of any kind.

He was kind enough to refer me to a Professor Sui Chong at the Singapore University. Dr. Chung was an expert on the economy of Singapore and would welcome a discussion with me on expanding it. He was a godsend as he was fluent in several languages and knew the most knowledgeable folks in Singapore who could give me advice on our projects. I asked him about the labor market and he said that was perhaps the least of my problems as there was a wealth of people looking for work. He advised me to work with the Striates Labor Co, as they would provide the best and most trustworthy workers. I told him I needed to first clear jungle to start the plan for our livestock project. He became very excited about our plan and offered to help us in any way he could. It was obvious to me that he could sense good things in the colony's progress if we were successful. I asked him where was the best place to obtain beef cattle and pigs to start our livestock. I figured chicken would be readily available here in Singapore and on surrounding islands. He immediately suggested Australia for the cattle and pigs. I asked him about slaughterhouses, and he said I should pursue that info again in Australia. I think this might be a tremendous boost to many people but to increase the development of the Lee Industries capability, we must start somewhere.

Cracking with the plan. I went to Straits Labor Co. and hired 25 men to start the clearing of the jungle for the livestock project. I kept Dr. Lee in the loop, and he pretty much gave me carte blanche to proceed. The labors came with a Chinese foreman who I liked and we hit it off right from the get go. I moved around in my jeep always with my gunner and realized that travel in the rough jungle and even in the cleared areas called for a horse to navigate quickly and safely. I was also warned that bringing horses on the property might also attract tigers. Good grief, didn't I have enough problems without having to worry about the *big* pussycats! I bought two horses from a local breeder, a stud and a mare to start our stable of horses. I found a gent on our staff working on the rubber plantation who was a knowledgeable horse guy, so started our stable. The clearing of the ancient jungles went slowly until I recommended control burning. That sped things up a little but was not too effective in the damp jungle. My gunner shot and killed our first tiger during our third day of clearing. Our laborers weren't too keen to continue, but our supervisor convinced them to continue with a small increase in salary that I authorized.

I headed for Australia to buy the first of our livestock with the guidance of Sui Chong who was familiar with several ranchers in Australia. I ended up with ten beef cattle, cows, and two bulls, and fifteen pigs. They were to be surface shipped to arrive in twenty days. That gave us enough time to clear some five hectares to make room for the cattle and pigs. We built pigsties and stockyards for the cattle, and when the animals arrived we were ready for them though in a pretty primitive fashion! Once settled, the bulls did their thing and we soon had ten calves to continue the growth of our herd. We planted two hectares in hay and corn for feed for both critter types. We built large chicken coops more like small warehouses and started our chicken farm. On a suggestion from a professor from the university, we poured concrete slabs for our pigs. This kept their hooves off the ground and prevented all sort of problems for the pigs. The slaughterhouse went up quickly as we aimed to begin supplying meat to the Singapore population as soon as feasible. Our goal was for a 75 head cattle count, 50 hogs, and 700 chickens. We figured this would give us enough animals to continue a supply of meat to the market and a replenishment source. We continued our jungle clearing to provide proper land for the cattle.

When we had our livestock enterprise pretty well established, I was anxious to see what we had in that hole with the weeping of gas and oil. I needed help. During my visit to Australia, while out on the town with a rancher from whom I made the livestock purchase, we ran into an old friend of his who I thought was a rummy and looked and talked like one. He had worked in the oil and natural gas fields in Australia off and on for twenty years. I told him about our sinkhole of oil and gas, and he became very interested. He asked if he might come and visit our location in Singapore, and I said yes as I desperately needed someone with the expertise to commercialize these products as part of our enterprises. He agreed but wanted all expenses paid for travel and lodging and experiments of our potential.

It seemed like an inexpensive way to get started, so I agreed to his request. Back at the ranch, Dr. Lee was now, because of me, having to dig into his reserved cash to finance our enterprises. He had a number of bankers who were friends and were encouraging the expanding of Singapore's economy and were more than willing to make necessary loans to Dr. Lee as needed. I was curious why some of the ideas that I was championing had not been tried in time past. Dr. Lee and his senior staff met each Monday morning and then following the meeting Dr. Lee would depart for the hospital and would normally not have a presence at the company until the following Monday. In effect the company was being run by some six senior staff who were more than content to maintain the status quo. Dr. Lee had agreed to allow me to visit with him in his home once a week as long as I brought Abby along! I was keeping him up to speed as what I was doing with his money and company. I was a maverick and my actions were not terribly appreciated by these dormant six gents. I needed their support as my actions demanded the full cooperation of all facets of the co. I was determined to win these gents over to my new, and I believed were new and dynamic, actions.

I have been amiss for failing to keep the reader advised as to what Abby was up to as I was having so much fun setting Dr. Lee's company on its ear! She was up to her ears working with the kids at the hospital. She was gaining the respect of all the doctors and nurses because of her brilliance in childcare and surgical skills in addition to her dynamic work ethic. Home life was wonderful. I had never been so happy, even when flying my fighters off an aircraft carrier for Uncle's Navy. My rummy friend from Australia, Jock Wagner, arrived and I put him in our jeep and with our gunner aboard we headed out to my sinkhole. He didn't say a word just scouted around the hole, sniffing and taking some reading on a handheld piece of equipment that I didn't understand. Without a word for about an hour, he sniffed and looked at the surrounding jungle and finally said, "Let's go somewhere to talk!" I took him to my office and shut the door and told my secretary to not disturb us. I still wasn't sure if this guy was a rummy or just looked like one. I soon found that this old guy was a walking genius as to anything having to do with natural gas and oil. The physical makeup look of him was a facade and was a part of his personality. He started out his discourse with the statement that, "I don't like tigers!" That sort of cleared the air and he started on his unrehearsed presentation that, "I am going to make you rich!" Wow, what a great attention getter! We went uphill from there as he stated that his early observations were that we were sitting on a gold mine of oil and gas of the finest quality that he had seen in a long time! He said his remarks were maybe a tad too expansive early on but from his early examination suggests that the products look to be remarkably superior.

He said that if we let him proceed he would arrange for all the equipment needed for drilling and only wanted to own a part of the final products. He said that before he proceeded with the drilling business he wanted an area cleared for 300 feet around the hole, which would become the drilling site. I told him to slow down. I had to get approval before we started to obtain the drilling equipment, etc. I told him I did not believe that Dr. Lee would give Jock a part of the products but would reward him handsomely if he could under salary proceed with the necessary preparations and drilling. I asked what sort of support structure would be needed once the oil and gas started to flow if we were lucky?

Dr. Lee backed me up and said proceed. He agreed to pay Jock a nice retainer betting on the drilling success of bringing the products to the surface. Jock told me we would need storage for the oil and a converter facility to change the natural gas to LNG (Liquid Natural Gas). If successful with bringing the products to the surface, much piping for oil and gas would be need to transport the products to storage and liquefaction.

Dr. Lee told me it would mean another trip to the bank, but he had faith that our efforts would bring big rewards, and if nothing else we were bringing life to the land that had been lying dormant for many years.

More land to clear was keeping my original labor hire busy, and we had added a few more laborers to our original hiring. They worked hard and worked fast but kept their eye on the jungle and the readiness of the gunners as they worked. Jock accepted the retainer that Dr. Lee provided and the open credit he provided for Jock to procure the equipment that he needed. He found a drilling rig and equipment that he needed from a Philippine oil company in Borneo. Seven weeks passed before our equipment arrived by ship from Borneo. The jungle had been cleared to Jock's satisfaction as he said he needed elbow room for his equipment, managers shack, and protection from the tigers! In just a few days, he had the rig ready to start. He had been a tad perturbed as he did not have a full-time, fully trained crew. Actually he trained the crew he needed from our labor pool. There were some surprisingly adept men in the pool who took to Jock's training with relish.

HOORAH! Stop the presses, Abby announced that she was pregnant. Now how could that happen? I knew, but was keeping it a secret. Abby's mom was as excited as anyone else besides me! Abby as a doc said she thought it was true a while before she took the pregnancy tests at the hospital. Dr. Lee was as excited as any one and was already acting like a godfather before he had even been asked. He was, but more later!

Laurie and Lisa were identified several months later. Mike Scott took full credit for twins as his mother had been a twin back in Scotland years ago. I was enjoying it all and simply just walked around with a large smile.

We built a small mobile office for Jock, which was most pleasing for him. He had advised us that if our potential oil and gas reservoir was as large as he suspected, he anticipated a number of wells would be needed. I enjoyed his enthusiasm but kept my fingers crossed hoping he was correct. With the drilling rig in place, Jock started the drilling. I assumed that in a few days we would hit gold, but I had a lot to learn about drilling. Our drill was an old one with none of the whistles and bells that we would have in later rigs.

We put the drilling on the clock and waited for the miracle that Jock said was coming! Lo and behold, the natural gas came first and Jock used a technique to put the gas aside temporarily while he continued drilling deeper for oil. This all took several weeks, but I can describe it in just a paragraph of writing. To say we had a celebration when the first oil arrived would be a major understatement. All of our staff from the entire complex plus the office staff and day laborers hurriedly arrived at the scene to watch the first burst of oil from Lee Well. No! Dr. Lee arrived late as he had surgery scheduled that he had to do before he hurriedly came to the site. (Side note, I wonder what the tigers thought about all these folks on their land screaming and yelling while the erupting oil was making a mess.)

With the first successful drilling, Dr. Lee's bankers sat back with large smiles showing their contentment. Jock had told me that if he was successful in bringing up the products, the piping and storage would be needed chop-chop or we might lose some of our product. I admit we (I) had been remiss to start the construction of piping and storage of the oil and piping and a conversion facility to liquefy the gas. Beyond that I had not addressed the transportation requirements to get our products to customers. With some urgency we started the piping, oil storage, and gas liquefying facility. Though the gas and oil had been brought to the surface, I had failed to start the marketing of our oil and LNG. I think in the back of my mind I wasn't 100% sure that Jock could pull it off. I needed help on the marketing. I found ready customers here at home for the oil and LNG though the ready customers needed some time to prepare their business to use the products.

With the advice and information from our university economic experts, I packed my bags and headed for the Philippines, Hong Kong, and Japan. I had some cultural differences with our senior staff and some reluctance from the boss to approach the Japanese. The hate and discontent toward the Japanese was very slow to fade from these previously occupied countries. Hong Kong was pleased and said after they examined samples of our product and were satisfied to its quality they would probably be ready to buy. The Japanese were not as re-luctant and said they would buy all the oil and NLG that we could supply; they even offered to send their tankers to pick up the products in that we had no ships of our own for delivery. I was starting to feel pretty stupid about the preparations needed to handle our products. Jock got into the act and really gave me a tongue lashing for my lack of preparations. My excuse was lack of knowledge and no experience working with oil and LNG products. I decided I was an idea man working hard with someone else's money to try and make our industry successful. Jock announced that we were sitting on a major oil and gas field. His preliminary estimate was that we could be pumping for fifty more years. More good news: The quality of our oil and gas were in the upper echelon of quality in petroleum products!

I met with Dr. Lee and gave him this great news and passed on Jock's suggestion that we continue to drill in additional locations near our present well. I told him he also should consider leasing ships to carry our products to market, primarily Japan. He was thoughtful and said he realized the importance of moving our idea along, but he said he was conservative, and as the heir to his family's wealth, he felt that some caution in expansion was due. I could hardly disagree with his thoughts and said I would be sure to keep him advised before I did any more expansion with his dollar!

He asked me to sit down and listen. He told me how pleased he had been with my actions since joining his company. He said he had thought that I could be a valuable addition to his staff but hadn't realized the energy I would bring to the company and the great ideas that I had to grow the company's assets. He had started me off with a moderate salary with the auto and house provided. He now gave me an excellent bonus in respect to the idea and action to bring oil and gas to the company's assets. I was embarrassed but readily accepted his generosity! He stated that he had offered me the position in his company in order to keep Abby in Singapore to be his associate and later to take over his practice. I told him that was not a secret but had been obvious to me from the get go!

I told Jock he could drill one more well and so advised Dr. Lee who offered no objection. Jock said he had worked up a primitive map of where he thought more wells should be drilled. The pattern was a circle of locations around the original well. The radius of the circle from the center well was 200 yards. Wow! This made for a large area, and Jock said he needed more clearing to have room to operate and protection from our tiger friends. I showed the pattern to Dr. Lee and he said he thought it looked ok but he again advised moving slowly and conservatively. I realized now that I was such an experienced drilling man that we would need more storage for our oil and more capability to convert the natural gas to LNG. Interestingly, LNG takes up 1/600th of the space for storage than natural gas! More expense, but Dr. Lee was spending a bit more of his time with his bankers who were more than willing to help him money wise! The bankers could see the handwriting on the wall that Lee Industries was on the brink of a major expansion in its business and they were anxious to ride that wave to fruitarian.

I should mention that in spite of Dr. Lee's conservatism, he agreed to put ten more hectares into rubber plant production. He was comfortable with rubber production. Additionally, the professors at the university suggested an improved process to extract the tin from the ore that we were bringing to the surface for our conversion facility. With all of our expansion, we were increasing our labor complement. We were finding individual laborers, who though poorly educated, were bright, smart, inquisitive, and hard-working. They were emerging as leaders who most certainly were making my job easier as I was finding folks that I could put in charge and not worry about the job being accomplished.

In the year that had passed, our livestock program was progressing. Our herd of beef cattle had grown to fifty animals and the bulls should have been given medals for duty above and beyond. Our pig population had grown to thirty-five pigs; some had become big sows that weren't very friendly to someone close at hand on foot. The chickens had exploded and were the only facet of our livestock that was using our new slaughter-house. There was a great market for chicken from among the Asian population of Singapore. Our new packing house presented our butchered chicken in a clean and attractive packaging rather than the usual dead hanging chickens.

One of most perplexing problems was the transportation of our oil and LNG products to foreign customers, primarily Japan. We did not own any ships and had to rely on expensive rental vessels. I was never comfortable for turning our very valuable product over to rental vessels with sometime questionable crews. I remember lying awake nights wondering how we could solve the problem of transportation as we were losing money on getting our product to market. Let's face it, we needed our own ships! I was reluctant to approach Dr. Lee with this very expensive requirement, but after I had a study done by our economists showing cost and supply ratio with and without our own ships, it became very obvious that we were losing money by renting instead of buying our own ships. The cost of ship leasing cut deeply into the profits we could have realized if we had our own ship(s). I addressed this need with Dr. Lee. My recommendation was that I fly to the States and visit with shipbuilders on the Gulf Coast. I suggested we needed a combination type ship that could carry all of our products. That included rubber, tin, meat, and oil and LNG. I thought it was feasible, but I needed to sit down with ship designers and discuss our needs. Dr. Lee agreed and asked me to use caution as we were embarking on an investment in a ship that would require an elevated budget that would show a loss for the time it would take us to pay off the price of a ship. The data from our own economist showed that with the continued flow of our oil and LNG that we could afford a ship and could pay off the costs rather quickly. We needed to insure that we didn't lose our markets, especially with Japan! I think I mentioned that Japan would lease ships to us for our oil and LNG.

While I was the big time spender with someone else's money, Abby was making waves of her own. Her practice was booming as she was in constant demand for pediatric surgery for many poor kids that couldn't afford the prices. The wealthy patients also wanted her for work with their kids as Abby was considered the best in the hospital right along with Dr. Lee. While in bed one evening, Abby told me she had a secret for a project she couldn't solve. She said she wanted a private pediatric clinic where she could work with her patients. She wanted to provide pro bono work for the poor kids and thought she could finance the business from her work with more affluent patients. She was certain that would work, but her main problem was building the clinic as she didn't know where the money would come from. The problem seemed simple to me as her mentor was loaded, loved her, though I was trying to spend his money as fast I could.

We invited Dr. and Mrs. Lee to dinner and Abby presented her problem to him. He was of course very interested and said he thought that he might be able to finance the project via donations from his wealthy friends in Singapore. He knew them all, and as a former president of the Royal Singapore Golf and Country Club, he believed he had a potential audience. He said he would start a program to raise the money. He thought that he and Sara (Mrs. Lee) could through their social contacts put on meetings and social gatherings to help raise the money. He had one caveat: Abby had to attend all meetings and social events and explain her plan. I thought he was a smart old devil bringing a beautiful, young, well-known, auburn-haired lady to sell her clinic plan.

Armed with as much information as I could contain from Jock, our economic experts and guidance from my professor friends from the university, I flew to New Orleans and rented a car. I hoped that my Singapore driver's license would keep me out of jail. Jock had via mail and phone had set me up with a Mr. Tom Hogan who was the Operations Officer for Andersen Shipbuilders, my initial contact with a shipbuilder. Mr. Hogan seemed very happy to meet with me, but I assumed he saw me with dollar signs in his eyes. I explained the purpose for my visit and he broke out artist drawings of combination ships. I told him that our primary focus was on oil and LNG and our secondary aim was for the other cargo items. He understood but kept taking me back to bulk cargo designs that did not feature oil and LNG.

When I left his office, I checked into a local motel that had a bar and restaurant attached. You guessed it, I had dinner there and then sat in the bar for a night cap, and at the bar I started a conversation with a nice-looking gent who told me he was an engineering designer for ocean going ships. His name was Jack Everting. I told him my problem and he allowed he might be able to help me. He had a small office nearby and invited me to stop by on the morrow and he thought he might be able to help me with my inquiries. It was certainly worth a try. He was the greatest thing since sliced bread. He readily understood my problem. He said that combination ships were a rarity. He asked if I thought that we would be expanding to more oil and LNG. I told him yes. He said that we, that is Lee Industries, would make a better investment in just oil and LNG vessels rather than a combination of fuels and dry goods. He said that if he were in our business he would concentrate on the fuel vessels rather than the dry good combination vessel in that we were going to make our greatest profits from the fuel not the dry goods. He recommended that we, in addition to a fuel cargo ship, buy or lease a smaller vessel to carry our dry goods.

He made a lot of sense and I wished he could speak to Dr. Lee and explain the rationale of avoiding a combination ship versus a fuel-only ship due to the profit considerations. He said if I liked he would introduce me to a local shipbuilder in Pascagoula who could help me out. Would I? Is the Pope Catholic? This guy was a godsend, and as I talked with him I realized that I was a babe in the woods in regard to shipbuilding and design considerations. He offered to join me in my meeting with his recommended shipbuilder. I hadn't offered this gent a penny but hoped that perhaps the shipbuilder to whom he was going to introduce me might just provide this gent with a finder's fee if we bought from the builder. Not my worry, but I did want to see this very knowledgeable and friendly guy get something for his advice and guidance to me.

We made an appointment later that day with Bill Clifford, President of Clifford Shipbuilding company. I liked him immediately as my first impression was that he was honest and straightforward, no fooling around, just knowledgeable and common sense thinking. This was the start of a long and profitable relationship between Cliff and I and Lee Industries and Clifford Shipbuilding, and I was the guy who kicked it off! I must not take all the credit as I would probably not have ever found Cliff if it hadn't been for Jack Everting.

Jack introduced us and I gave Cliff a thumbnail sketch of my problem. Cliff agreed that if we anticipated substantial growth in the output of our fuel products to keep with the ships designed to carry oil and LNG as the profits there were head and shoulder above the announced dry food products. Additionally, the food products did not take up as much space and the return profit on the sale of those products was considerably below the return on fuel. I explained to Cliff my company's situation, that is, that we had just discovered the large amount of oil and gas and had just recently decided to drill a second well. He asked what were the dry goods that we were considering for sea transport. I told him that we had started up a livestock program with beef cattle, pigs, and chicken. He asked how soon would we be ready to transport those products to foreign ports for sale. I told him that we thought we were about a year away from selling these products outside of Singapore. He suggested that we put the need to transport those products on the back burner and concentrate on the moneymakers of oil and LNG, which were much closer to transporting than the livestock. I told him that we had tried the transport of oil and LNG on leased ships and he thought we were simply wasting a lot of money that way. He told me the same thing that others had told me so I was now a believer...

I think these guys were starting to realize I was a novice in this business though they treated me with respect and patience. I later thought that maybe they were setting me up for a big loss of revenue, but later I put those thoughts out of my head as these guys were straight shooters. I am not suggesting they weren't good businessmen and surely viewed me as a good potential long-time customer. That is exactly what we became. Cliff was pretty straight with me. He said flat out that combination ships never seemed to work out especially if one has an excellent output of product it is smart to put oil into bunker ships and LNG into LNG domed ships. It also makes for more simplicity in loading and in offloading.

Great, I was sent to the Gulf Coast to check on the price of a combination ship, now I am being, I think honestly, guided to two ships rather than one. I obviously need to talk to the boss, Dr. Lee. I figured the best way to convince Dr. Lee was to have Cliff talk to him. I asked Cliff if he would be available to travel to Singapore for that task. Surprisingly, he said ok. I think the potential of Lee Industries to become big time in the delivery of fuel had gotten Cliff's attention.

While the iron was hot, I arranged a flight for Cliff and I to fly home. The meeting with Dr. Lee was a good one as Dr. Lee listened to me, as to my personal opinion of Cliff, and Dr. Lee almost immediately warmed up to this gent. Prices were now discussed with a price tag of $1.5 million for a simple bunker ship for oil and $2 million for the more complex LNG ship. Dr. Lee, God bless him, did not blink an eye but suggested to Cliff that he anticipated the order of more ships as the fuels were flowing well out of our wells as Jock advised. Spectacular. Our continued communications with Japan was for non-wavering commitment to send all the oil and LNG that we could! I began to realize that Dr. Lee had had some good deeply informative discussions with his bankers and was convinced that they would back him on loans for ships. Everyone involved believed we were sitting on a gold mine of fuel and that there was an excellent market for our products. Dr. Lee and the missus laid on a very nice social engagement for Cliff, inviting the key folks from our staff and his banker friends. Abby and I were of course invited as were a number of Dr. Lee's friends. Wow, before Cliff returned to Pascagoula, Dr. Lee signed the contract for the two ships for delivery in six months. This was all great, but there were other needs before we started operating ships. We needed pier space and perhaps more importantly crews for the two ships. Back to the drawing board. We (Dr. lee and I) approached his friends in the government and explained our need for pier space; in fact the boss said he wanted to buy a pier or construct one. The government agreed that they would sell waterfront property to Dr. Lee with the requirement that they approve the design and the caveat that they reserved the final approval of the pier. We advised them that the pier would be the recipient of oil and LNG to be loaded into our ships for transport to our markets. This would require some rather sophisticated equipment to be installed on the pier and considerable piping to bring our product to the pier. This didn't seem to bother them at all as I read between the lines and realized these government folks were friends of Dr. Lee and were aware of the potential wealth we would be bringing to Singapore.

While I was gone, Dr. Lee had authorized Jock to put in a third well and the results were the same exciting occurrence we had had before. The pier was underway with little problems, as was the piping to the pier from our oil storage and LNG plant. We had been smart and built our first LNG plant with the capability of adding more modules as we progressed converting the natural gas to LNG. We also continued to build storage tanks for our oil as we couldn't ship it as fast as the wells were delivering the product. (Tough problem!)

Ships were coming and we decided we wanted to form our crews for the two ships to be ready to board when the ships are ready for delivery. I decided that I wanted to become involved with selecting our crews. Surprisingly, Jock had a good working knowledge of crew selection from his many years' involvement with the industry. He recommended we contact a Philippine company: Luzon Ocean Personnel Company. It was a great recommendation and we worked with them for a number of years. I flew to Manila with Jock and we made arrangements to have the crews on site in Pascagoula upon ship delivery. I wanted Jock with me as we were given the opportunity to inspect the two ships before accepting delivery. Jock was obviously worth his weight in gold, and Dr. Lee recognized his value to our company by setting his salary as one of the highest in the company. I wasn't hurting either as the boss was quick to recognize our efforts in entering into the very rewarding business of oil and LNG.

I had not forgotten our rubber, tin, and livestock (meat) sales. We decide to concentrate on local sales of the meat to customers in Singapore and the surrounding territories as we could deliver those meat products by surface transportation. The tin and rubber would have to find room topside storage on our ships. In my discussions with Cliff, I pointed out our need to get the tin and rubber to customers by sea. He said in the construction of the oiler he would allow a small section of topside storage and some bunker storage. DAMN, we were getting a combination ship of sorts after all.

I invited the two new Captains with their first mates and Chief Engineers to Singapore from the Philippines to provide them with guidance as to what to expect from Lee Industries and what I expected in good seamanship and leadership. We selected a date for rendezvous at the building site in Pascagoula for the crews with Jock and me to accept the ships and to sail with them to Singapore. Requirements were falling into place with the crew, pier, and ships. I asked Dr. Lee to allow me to establish a safety division in our company to oversee all facets of safety in our enterprises. I hired a local gent who was experienced with shipping and engineering. A crew was formed by him and me. I selected some of those earlier employees who had demonstrated good skills in our business.

I have ignored my family in this writing while deeply involved in our shipping events. Abby was moving along quite well with her pregnancy, at least that is how I viewed the pregnancy progress as a new potential father. She later told me she had some scary moments and pains that were very new to her and that she didn't want those items to burden me. What a gal! How in the world had I been so lucky to come halfway around the world to find her! With the capabilities of her hospital, they had determined that Abby was going to deliver twin girls.

Happy days! You would think that Dr. Lee was the parent as he was so excited over the news! We were both very pleased that we would have twins in our family. We started working on names for these two additions.

Back to work! We continued with our drilling, and as Jock had predicted, the amount and quality of our products continually exceeded even Jock's anticipation. We finished the circle of wells around our original well with a total of nine wells including Lee No. 1. Jock without wasting any time started looking over the industry's land on where to start new drillings. After our first experience of buying ships, it soon became obvious that we would need additional ships to move the increasing supply of oil and LNG from our storage and conversion facility to our ever-thirsty customers in Japan. I was off to Pascagoula to meet with our friend Cliff. We had become pretty close friends by now and he entertained me royally. He had a family of a lovely wife and two sons off in college. I reminded him that he had said he could adjust the prices on the two new ships we wanted to order. He agreed and said six months to delivery. I asked if that time could be reduced as we were awash in fuel. He said he could, but only at the original prices. I agreed as we needed the ships. We had found on our first trip to Japan that the fuels had sold took care of half of the price we had paid for each ship. We were making the most money from the LNG, but the price paid for the oil was not to be sneezed at. In looking ahead, it appeared that we would probably need to order our ships at two LNG ships for each oil bunker ship. As our activity on the pier increased, we created a pier gang whose job it was to load the fuels on our ships and handle the arrivals and departures of our ships. With our fleet starting to increase, we decided that we could operate two ships on one side of the pier, but as we looked into the future, it appeared that there might be times when we would have two ships on each side of the pier. We added the equipment to the pier to be ready for fueling up to four ships at a time. Ships require preventative maintenance. If maintenance is not done before problems appear, problems multiply and ships are likely to be put out of service and into a maintenance status. You cannot make money with a ship if it is out of service for maintenance. Singapore has a superb maintenance and repair facility for ship repair and maintenance. We early on anticipated that we would need preventative maintenance for our ships so we established an agreement for maintenance with that organization. We established ship availability to do preventative maintenance work before major problems appeared. Most of the problems that tie ships up occur in the propulsive systems rather than hulls. We found that being ready for problems before they occurred paid off handsomely and was very cost effective.

# Chapter 6

# Lee Time

This ship stuff is interesting and fun but nothing like Abby's birth of our twins. It was of course much more fun for me as all I had to do was hold her hand, tell her to be brave, and watch the procedure that I had started! Abby was a real trooper and delivered with pretty short labor. I of course knew all about this birthing business so I could make judgments about the procedure and Abby's involvement. Actually she did really fine and delivered two beautiful girls; both had reddish fringe hair like their mom. What did I have to offer? Nada, just good health and good teeth if they ever grow any. This babble to let off the steam that I worked up while Abby did her thing in a beautiful and pretty easy way. HOORAY! Two for one—twins! Little did I know that these two beautiful creatures were going to rob me of sleep for the next several months. We had agreed on names as Laurie and Lisa, with Laurie being the older by eight minutes.

We found that we had a fine market for our livestock meat production. Singapore and surrounding islands were hungry for meat so there was no reason to add our meat products to our ships. We continued to develop our fuel output and continually leaned towards LNG rather than bulk oil. There was a better market for the LNG and the profit realized was the main reason we started to put the most effort into LNG. It was more expensive to process as the natural gas has to be cooled considerably to put it into a liquid state, but our customers in Japan preferred LNG over bulk oil. Our fleet was increasing as we now three years later, had ten LNG ships, and only five bulk oil carriers. We had become one of the prime industries in Singapore with our fuel products. Dr. Lee simply smiled a lot. The fuel business was pretty much running itself with a minimum of effort from me. I kept looking at the large amount of land that

Lee Industries owned and decided I needed to spend some time developing that land. Our wells took up quite a bit of land as it was necessary to provide cleared land for not only the wells but for all the equipment that was needed to operate the wells successfully. Our livestock area had been increased primarily to provide grazing area for the cattle, but the pigs and chickens did not need a great deal of land to operate. With all this invested activity, our greatest need was for labor. Much of the fuel business required skilled labor that we had to train ourselves. The livestock was not as labor demanding as was our rubber and tin production. I recalled from several trips to Hawaii while growing up that sugar cane with sugar mills were very productive as a money making proposition. Sugar cane fields need quite a bit of land to be productive and we had it! This became our next challenge. I sent two of our senor staff to Hawaii to scope out the requirement that we needed to meet to get into the sugar business. They came back loaded with data but most importantly had hired a Chinese Hawaiian to be our guru in the development of the sugar business. Again, we started with land clearing and the construction of a sugar mill. Our new sugar expert advised us to save all of the sugar cane residue, and with simply reprocessing, it can be used for feed and fertilizer, the food for the cattle and pigs. Within a year, we were in the sugar business. Again, the market was right here in home and we found that our Japanese customers would take sugar also for distribution in their country where land for any product that needed land was in short supply. We stored the sugar on deck of the LNG ships in sealed containers that traveled well.

Dr. Lee called me into his office and showed me his profit and loss statistics and he said that thanks to me he was a very rich man. He said that as he was sailing along with his income from rubber and tin he was making an excellent living, but with the addition of more rubber production plus oil, LNG, and sugar I had made him a very wealthy man. He was always a very generous guy especially in anything in that Abby was involved. As my wife Abby was involved. Dr. Lee said he wanted to reward me for what I had done for his company. I told him if he wanted to reward me, he could provide Abby with a first class children's clinic so she could expand her work and take over much of the load that he was carrying with his work with the kids. He thought that was a marvelous suggestion and made it so. A year later, Abby had her clinic and was funding its day-to-day operations by charging wealthy parents at cost and poor kids at pro bono. Dr. Lee provided my family and me with membership in the Royal Singapore Country Club as full-fledged members. He didn't stop there but gave Abby and me and the twins a brand new four-bedroom, three-bath home in the nicest district in the city. Our two servants came to the new home with us plus the YaYa that we had hired when the twins were born. Who said, "Ain't life grand!" Dr. Lee told me that thanks to his bankers, all our endeavors had been made possible plus he had paid back every loan and didn't owe them a cent. I thought he was making retirement noises, but that didn't happen for a few more years. I did not know how old he was as I found that as a "round eye" it was difficult to guess the age of my senior Chinese friends.

Life was good. I was married to the most beautiful girl in Singapore, who was a favorite of the community for her work with kids and for her bravery during the occupation. I found that whenever we went anywhere socially I was a sore thumb as Abby drew all the attention. That was fine with me as she had certainly earned the locals' love and respect. I think I was just the American who had fallen into a grand position because of Abby and Dr. Lee. It wasn't far from the truth. I was delighted to simply bask in her limelight!

The twins were three when Abby, in spite of her busy schedule, delivered a beautiful son who we named Richard after Abby's grandpa and brother. The twins loved their little brother and took care of him. He was a very well-loved little kid from his sisters, Abby, the YaYa, and don't forget the old man, me!

Now that the Lee Industries was running well and I had brought those old seniors into my personal circle of friends—they were getting rich also—I found time with my new membership in the country club to take up golf. I started out as a real duffer and like most early on golfers loved the game but couldn't seem to get very good at this most frustrating game.

Instead of taking to drink I hired the club pro to give me lessons. It was the smartest thing I ever did. This guy had been teaching golf for years and was the most patient man I think I had ever known. He would show me how to do something right and then led me through much time for repetition and practice until I became pretty good at that one facet of the game. After about six months with this guy, I became acceptable to play with my friends. I certainly never was going to win the club championship, but I was having fun and was no longer embarrassed by my score. Golf takes up a lot of time and to be good at it one must play frequently. I played frequently and was able to keep my business running well with the minimum of personal effort. We had trained a lot of people in the various disciplines required to run the company so I did not feel any guilt for the time spent on the course. I had become primarily a decision maker, and though I was called upon frequently I still had time for golf and family.

For the first time in my life I had put down roots with my family, my business, and my community. Nice feeling! The kids were growing like weeds and were all three bright, personable, and beautiful. I could only sit back with a successful family and job and smile. I kept saying to myself—be careful, whenever you are on such a high there is always the potential that all will change and come tumbling down. It didn't happen, instead more good things kept coming my way.

Dr. Lee remembered that when I first arrived in Singapore it was on an aircraft carrier and I was a junior bird man (fighter pilot). He said he always wanted to fly but never seemed to have the time to take lessons. He asked me if he bought an airplane would I teach him to fly. I of course told him of course, but I would need some refresher before I had confidence that I could teach him to fly. I did. He did and bought a Waco, single engine, four-seater. Nice bird with good legs to visit our Southeast Asian customers and be able to write off the bird for the company. He was a good student, eager to learn, and very safety conscious.

We were able to get his private license after he had logged thirty hours in the bird. He immediately told me he wanted to fly to Bali as he had never been there and had read extensively about that island. He asked if I would join him on that flight. I of course agreed to join him. We made the flight okay in daylight and landed okay. Dr. Lee had called ahead and made reservations at a swanky hotel on the water. He also had made an appointment with a real estate office to look at property. That office must have looked him up and found him to be very wealthy and treated him like a prince. I tagged along as he looked at property.

He insisted that the property be on the water and have at least four bedrooms, four baths, a pool, and all being on a main floor. The homes he was shown were in most cases beautiful and of course exceeded the minimum he had asked for. I realized, though he never said so, that he was looking for a retirement home in this luxurious area. I think that after his wartime guerilla lifestyle and happenings and a lifetime dedicated to helping children and now being very wealthy, he was planning to hang it all up and retire in style. (My thought was how was he ever going to slow down after all those years going at full speed.) I think his missus had a hand in all this as he always listened to her. Bali was beautiful, much like Hawaii as I remembered. I sort of swelled with pride at his actions to find a retirement home in this beautiful location. I realized, hopefully modestly, that I had quite a lot to do with making this available for him. That evening after a grand dinner and over a nightcap in the lounge he started a chat as to where his company was going in the future and what had happened in the past ten years. He gave me almost full credit for the progress the company had made. I reminded him that I had no money to invest and that the bankers would have probably thrown me out on my ear if I approached them for the millions of dollars that they had made available to him.

It was a pleasant evening and he topped it off by telling me he was going to retire in a year from his work with the hospital. He planned to hang on as owner of Lee Industries and would be available as necessary to interface with bankers as needed and make major decisions that I could or would not make. *What?* Where was he going with this conversation? He cleared the air by saying that at his retirement he would appoint me as president of Lee Industries! He would remain as owner and be available as needed. MY GOD, WOW! I nearly dropped dead with surprise and pleasure. Wait until I tell Abby! I told him how pleased I was with his plan and wondered how the senior folks on the staff would take the news? Would they be content to work for a "round eye"? Dr. Lee said he did not see that as a problem as they had been working for me the past ten years and all had become wealthy because of my decisions on developing the various aspects of Lee Industries!

I did not make any noises as to what my salary might be when I took over the job of president. I figured it was in bad taste to bring up that subject so soon after he broke the news of his decision. I didn't have to wait very long as he said he wasn't going to pay me a salary but would give Abby and me 25% of Lee Industries! Great and delightful news. I couldn't hardly wait to tell Abby.

Before we left Bali after our four-day stay, Dr. Lee made a down payment on a beautiful piece of property that any rich man would be more that content to own. He said that as soon as the property was available, he wanted to bring Abby and me and his wife, of course, for a vacation in his new digs. Surprisingly, I accepted his invitation.

The flight home was uneventful, but I was busting with pride and pleasure and I was so excited, I'm sure I added to the lift for the bird. I told Abby the news as soon as I arrived at our quarters. She took the news surprising quietly and said she thought it would happen some years ago. I suspect she had had whispers from her mentor named Lee. I believe she was more excited with the invitation of a vacation in Bali than with my good fortune. I did pique her interest when I told her that Dr. Lee was going to give us 25% of the company. That got her interest and I could almost read into her response as dollar signs for her clinic! With the 25% ownership of Lee Industries, Abby and I found that our income jumped very high indeed. We were becoming wealthy beyond any expectation that we had before. As expected, Abby asked that a portion of our new wealth be used to upgrade her clinic, which was relatively new, but she wanted expansion to open various wings to special illnesses of the kids. She also hired several additional doctors with whom she was involved to further expand her clinic's capabilities. She continued to offer her clinic's service to the wealthy patients of Singapore at fair prices but not at the pro bono she offered the poor.

Her compassion was bigger than her beauty and the little kids of Singapore were the beneficiaries of her generous heart. Our new founded wealth brought us a higher social standing in of the city. We over the years became very active in the country club, both as members of committees promoting club activities. We also were invited to join the embassy social circuit, which got us involved with Singapore's happenings and with other Southeast Asian countries. These social activities were good for my business and Abby's reaching out to wealthy folks' kid's health needs.

The twins had reached their teens and were making big noises of following in their mom's footsteps as doctors and joining their mother in her clinic. I think Abby was a good talker and recruiter. Richard was still a 9-

year-old terror driving his sisters to great anguish with his teasing and tricks against them.

Dr. Lee as always kept his word, and Abby and I spent a delightful week in Bali with the boss and his wife. By the end of that week, I think Abby had her eye on Bali as a great retirement spot. I told her I didn't think she would ever retire and give up her work with the kids of Singapore.

I unexpectedly was elected president of the country club. Quite an honor for a non-Singaporean. It certainly wasn't because of my golf scores, and I believed it was because of my rather famous spouse, a knighted war hero, a savior of many Singapore children, and the most beautiful auburn-haired lady in the joint! We didn't refuse the position, in fact I relished it. It certainly didn't hurt my business dealings with the locals nor the amount of money I lost on the golf links. It of course didn't hurt my relations with the U.S. Embassy as they were pleased that an American had risen to such a status in Singapore. I was occasionally called upon to discuss small problems that came up with U.S.-Singapore relations. It didn't hurt my relations with the Embassy staff as we were on a very comfortable relationship.

Dr. Lee did as he promised and retired to Bali leaving me in charge as president of Lee Industries. The oil and natural gas continued to flow as Jock had predicted and our fleet of ships was keeping busy delivering our product not only to Japan but also to South Korean who was on an economy busting surge now that peace had been established in the area. We were making some inroads to bringing in Hong Kong as a customer of all our products as Hong Kong was also exploding economically. I had been able, now that we had the Waco to contact potential customers closer to home in Jakarta, Kuala Lumpur, and Phnom Penh.

The twins were accepted as medical students at the Royal Singapore Hospital where their mother had trained and Richard was an "A" student at the local high school. The twins were making noise to do their residencies at Stanford, again following in their Mom's footsteps. I wonder if Richard might join the U.S. Navy and become a fighter pilot, but I digress, wishful thinking!

After all these years, Abby decided that she wanted to take a vacation to Scotland to visit the old Sod and to visit her aging grandfather who still was alive and quite well in Scotland. The kids were all busy with their studies and so were not going with us. Abby's mom and dad decided that in spite of slowing down, they wanted to make the trip home one more time. We flew on British Airways from Singapore to New York and then on to Edinburgh. A long flight but the drinks were good as was the service. There was no one to meet us, so we took a train for an hour to Penicuik in the Pentland Hills area. This was the early home for the Scott family and the resident town for Abby's grandpa. This was my first visit to Scotland and I looked upon the trip as a wonderful renewal of family history for Abby's family. Grandfather Scott was an old stooped gentleman who in his day had been a Colonel in the Highland's 12th Regiment and had fought considerably in the 1st World War. It became readily available that he had little love for Americans and just about said so. I was told that he had a bad experience in the war in a joint action with the Americans. I told him my dad had fought in WWI in the battles at Verdun and Chateau Thierry. That helped clear the air a tad. But I was going to have to prove myself to him before I would be accepted. Grandpa Scott made over to Abby as though she was lost and now found love. I understand Abby very closely resembled her grandmother who was now gone but well remembered by grandpa.

Grandpa's Scott's low opinion of me changed dramatically the next day as he insisted I go fishing with him. (I think you think I was going to catch the Lock Ness's Nessie, but that was certainly not to be.) He insisted that he knew the best fishing holes on their local pond and we sat at that hole with his rigs with nary a nibble. I asked him if he ever trolled for fish in this pond, and he swore that I didn't know anything about fishing as a Yank and to basically shut up and fish. Another hour went by and still not a nibble. I suggested that we re-rig our lines, but he would have not any of that. I final asked him if he would let me rig our lines for trolling but just for a little while. He, with a sneer, finally gave in as I think he was a tad embarrassed as to the failure to catch anything his way. So troll we did, and in our first sweep he got a good strike and he pulled in a beautiful bass. I followed in a minute or so and had a bigger fish than he had caught. We continued for another hour and ended with eight beauties. He insisted that he carry the fish to his local pub and show off our catch to his old drinking buddies while we put away a pint! He asked me not to tell his friends that we had caught this batch of fish while trolling as they never did that and he wanted to keep it a secret so he could try it by himself later. At the pub, he never told his friends that we had caught the fish while trolling. He was a hero and told his buddies he had taught me how to fish Scot style. (I doubt if the old Cogger ever told his drinking buddies the truth.) Needless to say his attitude toward this Yank totally changed and I was received into Grandpa's private circle of family like a lost soul. After our fishing expedition, we all enjoyed a grand week with Grandpa and his digs.

We flew home via the U.S. to New York and then a scooter flight to Boston where we were met by my mom and dad. They drove us to their home in North Scituate, Rhode Island where we were to spend another four days. I hadn't seen my folks since I left the Navy and made my way to Singapore. My folks and the Scots hit it off, which was nice to see as they came from totally different worlds. The glue that brought the two sets of parents together was Abby. She as always was with her delightful outgoing personality spent a lot of time relating to my folks what I had done in Singapore to bring major developments to

Lee Industries and in my spare time raise a family. I had of course related the experience that they had with the Japanese time, particularly Abby's role as an under-the-fence digger. I had been sending a few dollars to my folks to make life a tad easier for them and had been corresponding with them all these years. They lived modestly in the country at the edge of a beautiful wooded area. They were able to put us up okay and of course had lobsters the first night and my dad tried to scare Abby with her first lobster. He couldn't get a rise out of her as her life had made her pretty tough to any kind of fear, even to be chased by a lobster.

The flight home was uneventful but long. We flew to NY then to San Francisco and then the long flight to Singapore again with British Airways. I frankly slept most of the way. As a former aviator, sleeping on a passenger bird was a blessing to fly and do nothing except enjoy the service and sleep. Abby hated me as she was still a white-knuckle flyer!

Home was as always beautiful. Great to be in our home again and better yet to be with the kids after a rather long vacation. My first day back in the office was nice as I found that everything as still humming and running well (maybe they didn't need me anymore). Abby had a similar experience as her clinic was still there and running okay even without her guidance! The twins were still deeply involved with their studies, and Richard announced that he had made the decision to become a doctor and get rich! Lord save me, a family of four doctors plus Abby's dad, I was surrounded by medical folks! It would be great if I ever became ill! The girls announced that if Stanford was good enough for their mom and dad, that's where they had decided to go for their residency. It was a flippant announcement as I knew they has searched long and had for the best place for their continued studies.

Now that I was back to home, the office, the decision making, keeping Dr. Lee in the loop, I found that these responsibilities were hardly filling my day's work. Sure, golf was an important part of my life, but believe it or not I was a tad bored. My year as president of the country club had come to a close, and frankly after the past years of head down and charge I was bored! I had run out of challenges! What do you do when you are bored? Make more kids? No, Abby had done her duty and was knee deep in making the kid's world in Singapore a healthier place.

# Chapter 7

# The Pirates

I decided to do something exciting. I could only fly perhaps once a week on business travel and I couldn't even turn the old Waco over on its back, do a slow roll—I needed something to do! I bought a 42-foot boat that was perfect for entertaining, family weekends, to ride at anchor in some new and exotic cove, eat too much, chase Abby too much, and fish! Life began to look up, my morale improved, and I became a heck of a good fisherman up to the northwest fishing in the Strait of Malacca and when I wanted to splurge into the Andaman Sea. These waters were awash (dumb word) with fish just waiting for a sport fisherman such as me! The types of fish that were available are Spanish mackerel, barracuda, Bluefin, coral trout, pilot trevally, sailfish, and Wahoo. When I decided to take a longer trip up into the Andaman Sea for fishing with friends, we packed up lots of food and drink, brought our servants, and usually would make a five to six-day trip out of the cruise. We could sleep ten folks, a tad close but it was great fun and I was the skipper. I always made sure I had at least two crewmembers who were locals who knew the waters and where and how to fish and drop the hook for the night. I brought home lots of fish that I shared with my friends and neighbors. That is a fantastic part of the world, and with Abby along I had my own translator. Abby, in addition to her Scottish flavored English, also spoke Cantonese Chinese, Malaysian, and Japanese that she had learned the wrong way in camp!

We had the boat for about five years before something naturally bad occurred to put a big crimp on our fishing excursions. Pirates attacked another pleasure boat such as ours and killed the husband and kidnapped his wife and two kids. They were paid a large ransom, and the bastards put the wife and kids into a small boat and set them free to find their way to civilization. They were rescued by another boat that spotted them and brought them to safety in Singapore. The Navies and maritime police from the surrounding countries set up patrols and established regulations for boats such as ours. I quit going as far north as the Andaman Sea and restricted our outings to the Strait of Malacca. We stayed south for about six months and there were no more pirate attacks, so I applied to the police authorities in Singapore for licenses for an AR-15 and two 9 MM handguns and lots of ammunition! I was damned if those wild ass animals were going to keep me from my favorite fishing grounds. I taught Abby, the twins, and Richard how to use the 9 MMs. I saved the AR-15 for myself. Woe to anyone who tries to pirate my boat.

SURPRISE! It happened. On about the fourth trip I had made to the Andaman Sea, it happened. I had a group of friends aboard including my son, Richard. We noticed a very fast speedboat headed our way. This was the norm for the pirates to come at a victim at high speed then order the victim to stop making way, come alongside, and board quickly with about four to five pirates and take the occupants captive and possibly kill anyone who refused capture and take any other passengers into their boat as hostages. As soon as I spotted the bastards, I gave one 9MM handgun to a retired British colonel and one to Richard. I of course grabbed my AR-15. I told all my other passengers to go below and to keep quiet I as was going to fight the little buggers unless overwhelmed. I told Colonel Goddard and Richard to keep out of sight and not fire until I did. The speedboat came alongside, and I was making way at about five knots. They hollered in Malaysian for me to stop and be boarded. It was pretty obvious to me that they were going to take over my boat. I showed myself and pointed my weapon at them; they scrambled to grab their weapons and I opened fire with my AR-15. I emptied a magazine and inserted another magazine and continued to fire. I don't think they had a chance to get off a round at our boat, but I killed or wounded just about all of the eight men in the speed boat. The survivors raised their hands in surrender. I called to them to throw their weapons overboard.

We threw them a line and secured it to our stern and started to tow them to port in George Town, Malaysia. I put the Colonel on watch at the stern with his 9 MM and my AR-15 and we headed for George Town. I got on the horn and called the maritime authorities in George Town and related what had happened and told them I was heading into port towing pirates both dead and alive. Damn that was the most fun I had since flying and strafing, dropping napalm on the bad guys since the Korean War! I hadn't forgotten how to treat the bad guys! Damn, I bet they were surprised when I popped out with an AR-15. Richard and Colonel Goddard had both gotten a couple of rounds off but did not know if they had hit anything or not. When we arrived in George Town, the local authorities took the dead and alive pirates under control and asked me, the Colonel and Richard to sit and relate everything that had happened with the pirates. We did our thing and believed that we convinced the fuzz that we had acted properly. The authorities said that our action was the first to take out pirates and they believed us action would put a damper on any new pirate action. I doubted whether any pleasure boat fishermen would visit these waters without weapons. We were released with thanks for our action!

When we arrived back in port in Singapore, our action had been advertised in the local paper and folks made over us as though we were heroes. After Abby had made sure that we were not hurt, she lit into me for exposing Richard to the action. Richard said he was fine and that it had been wonderful to see his dad in action. That cooled Abby down a tad, but I was still a jerk in her eyes. Ain't life grand! I went back to fishing where I damn near wanted to fish. I was convinced that no pirate was going to fuss with "The Flying Low."

# Chapter 8

# Collision

We had a near collision with one of our oilers while en route from Tokyo to Singapore. She was empty but in ballast having off-loaded her oil at her destination. The incident occurred in the South China Sea at night. The first mate had the conn and was assisted by the helmsman who also acted as lookout, quartermaster, and lead helmsman. Merchantmen have small crews so the jobs on the bridge are shared especially at night during steady steaming. The helmsman reported a contact bearing off the port bow at about ten miles and the conn told him to keep an eye on his bearing. In about ten minutes the helmsman reported that the contact appeared to be about five miles out but had the same bearing about 120 degrees. Again, the conn told the helmsman to watch the contact for any bearing change. A few minutes later, the conn noted decreasing range and steady bearing on the contact. Our ship had the contact off his port bow so was privileged and the contact was burdened to make changes as necessary to avoid collision. As they closed, the first mate said, "To hell with it," and ordered full astern on the engine and turned the wheel full right to avoid a head on collision. Unfortunately, the contact did nothing to avoid collision and the two ships "rubbed" side together causing damage to both ships. The maritime hearing concluded that the burdened contact had no one on the bridge as the conning officer was back in the navigation shack having coffee. Our ship was exonerated, but we still had damage to our port side. We put our ship in the Singapore shipyard where we had a contract for maintenance and repairs. Lloyd's of London, our insurance company, concurred with the maritime decision that our ship was faultless and paid greatly in our favor for the ship repair. Nevertheless, having a ship out of operation was a big scheduling problem as we operated at close to full capacity with our ships to move our products that were constantly gushing out of the ground. Actually any time we put a ship into scheduled maintenance it ended to back up our flow of product to our customers. It frankly wasn't easy to juggle ship availability with customer needs.

# Chapter 9

# The Twins

The twins, Laurie and Lisa, continued to pretty much dominate our home life. As I became more affluent, I was able to send the girls to the best school in Singapore for young ladies. It was a Catholic girls' school run by the nuns of the Holy Mother Order. The girls were a wonderful mix of white, Chinese, and Malaysian kids. The white kids were mostly British subjects many whom had been in Singapore for most of their lives. The mix of nationalities provided all the students to broaden their knowledge and cultures of the various kids. It was a great democratic experience for all and fast friends were made. Both of our girls had inherited the great passion for helping others; in fact they had fortunately also inherited a lot of the beauty of their mother minus the auburn hair. The twins had announced in their junior year of school that they intended to become doctors and join their mother's clinic when they were able. Richard, their younger brother said, "They are dumb. I am going to become a doc and treat only rich people and get rich myself." This from the little guy the twins doted on when he was a baby. Life is indeed a mystery! It didn't take long for the girls to be accepted at medical school within the hospital. Their acceptance was a lock as they were Abby's kids and her kids could do no wrong at "her" hospital.

Fast forward, the twins graduated from medical school with honors as each tried to outdo their sister in friendly competition. During their junior year, they had applied to Stanford University for residency still following in their mom's footsteps. Abby just beamed with pride. Me too! When they were ready to fly to San Francisco for entry into Stanford, Abby and Richard and I accompanied the twins in order to get them settled. We rented a car in San Francisco and drove to Palo Alto. Upon arrival we checked in with the lovely lady who had rented an apartment to Abby and me years ago. She was still there, and when she saw Abby she cried and said of course she would rent the same apartment to the girls. After some discussions with Abby and strong guidance for the girls, we decided to buy them an automobile. In Singapore we of course, due to the British influence, drove on the left hand side of the road and the wheel was on the right side. The twins had learned to drive in Singapore and I insisted that they take driving lessons for the American style. Richard just laughed at his sisters! Abby visited the Stanford University hospital where she had done her residency and also worked for a year while I was finishing my two years at Stanford.

There was a doctor there who I had always suspected had the hots for Abby and of course I had been jealous, though Abby insisted he was no threat. The bugger was still there, and I'm sure when he saw Abby he was all excited again, or so said Abby. I ignored the whole business as Abby was mine and no one else could be a threat to our love. Abby, Richard, and I checked into a nearby hotel and tried (ha!) to get the girls started on the right foot. We were just in the way. Abby's reputation had preceded our arrival and the twins were able to waltz in as though they were old friends with the hospital and staff.

In that we were now on my old stomping grounds, the U.S., I wanted to touch base with my old friend Cliff at the shipyard in Pascagoula. We had been buying our ships from Cliff for a number of years and I always was present when we took delivery of a new ship. Cliff and I had become good friends and on one occasion he and his wife visited us in Singapore. That was his first visit to Southeast Asia and I think it was an eye opener and he saw as the potential markets for his ships. We arrived in New Orleans on a flight from San Francisco. It was Richard's first trip to the U.S. and he was awed by everything that he saw. I told him, "You ain't seen nothing yet." Cliff wined and dined us and gave Richard and myself a tour of the yard. Cliff had bid and won a contract to build ten amphibious landing ships for the U.S. Navy. He hoped that would be the start of a relationship with the Navy. Our next stop was Washington D.C. as the American Embassy folks had asked me to deliver a batch of personal documents to the State Department personnel. It was nothing official but did give us the opportunity for Abby and Richard to see Washington. We spent three days in Washington staying at the Mayflower and seeing the sights of the beautiful Washington buildings and monuments.

We flew from Washington to Providence, Rhode Island where I had been raised and my mom and dad still lived in the state. My dad met us, and as usual it was a nice welcome mostly centered on Abby and Richard. It was great to see my mom again as I hadn't been home very often in the past few years. Abby, of course, was the center of attention along with Richard. This was the first time that his grandparents had ever seen Richard so he also received lot of attention. Lobsters for dinner of course in Rhode Island. The Maine lobsters were a first for Richard as this was his first time in New England. They made a hit with him, and it was one of my most pleasant memories for me as I had darn near been raised on them. My folks took us on a tour of Rhode Island and we saw many places that I remembered from my youth. R.I. was a busy place during the Revolution, and many historic spots have been saved and locations maintained for tourists. Newport has been very evidently restored and is a highlight of any tour of R.I. Abby and Richard were not satisfied with our R.I. tour and insisted that we visit Boston, Lexington, and Concord plus the Freedom Trail as their interest in the Revolution had been peaked by the R.I. sights. My mom joined us as we drove to Boston and my family enjoyed the many historic sites from the pre-Revolution and the Revolution. Remember Abby and Richard had both been brought up under the leadership of the British Commonwealth so they were very interested in seeing the other side of the historic coin. The drive back to R.I. was full of questions from Abby and Richard, about the Revolution, many that my mom and I could not answer.

Abby and Richard both asked if we couldn't return home via Japan. I had no objection as I hadn't touched base with our customers there in quite a while. We flew from Providence to Chicago and then on to Tokyo. We planned to stay several days in Japan and were able to get into the U.S. military hotel based on my previous Navy service. I met with our several customers and they were most gracious and accommodating. No surprise as we had been pouring great fuel products into Japan for quite a long time. Abby, though she had a poor recollection towards her jailors during their incarnation, was quite sophisticated and realized how much our wealth had been caused because of the Japanese need for fuel. She was also in a great spot to practice the Japanese she had learned in the POW camp during the Japanese occupation of Singapore. I hadn't realized the extent of her language capability. As I have mentioned on several occasions, this lady was awash with many talents.

# Chapter 10

# Cultured Pearls

In the lobby of our hotel was a shop selling cultured pearls. Abby thought they were beautiful and I bought a necklace for her. They were quite a few yen less than natural pearls, but the beauty was about the same. I engaged the young lady who was running the pearl shop how the cultured pearls were created. She gave me a brochure explaining the process of inserting a grain of sand into the live young oysters and then over a period of several years the pearl was created in this shell around that grain of sand. As I was always interested in any type of business that I could install within Lee Industries. I asked the young lady if I could visit their factory. They offered a tour of their factory so I took one with Abby and she was as fascinated as I was. In discussions with the manager at the project, I explained my interest and asked if there was any reason I couldn't install the process in Singapore. She smiled and said that many folks had tried but all had failed. That of course got my dander up and caused me to have a deeper interest in the procedure. I asked the manager if he had any former Singaporean employees. He introduced us to a Chinese gentleman. It seems the gent had been an officer in the Chinese Army in China and had been taken prisoner by the Japanese during the war and had spent much of the war in a Japanese POW Camp. After the war he was released but chose to stay in Japan as he had fallen in love with and married a Japanese lady. I asked to meet him but honestly told the manager I was interested in trying to start a cultured pearl business and might offer this Chinese gent a job. The manager said he didn't think I would be successful, but he did not say he would not let me talk to and possibly hire this gent. Abby and I met with the guy, and Abby told him our thoughts about starting up a cultured pearl business. It seems he had been raised in Singapore but had moved to China with his family before the war and had joined the Army. He said he might be interested in moving back to Singapore as his grandparents still lived there. We told him that we did not have a pearl business but would he be interested in joining our company and installing and building such a business? He indicated his interest but needed to talk it over with his wife. He was naturally concerned with how his Japanese wife would be accepted in Singapore. I honestly told him that could be a problem that he should consider. He asked about salary and living accommodations, which I offered to him on a pretty lucrative scale. I challenged him by reminding him that his boss did not think we could be successful in getting such a business started. He didn't agree, but if he were unable, would I promise compensation if he failed. It was a heck of a complicated business start-up, but it was a challenge. I agreed with his request. Soon after we had returned to Singapore, he contacted me and said yes to our proposal.

We had a corner of our property in Queensland that was situated on a saltwater inlet that appeared to be a good site for our oyster caper. We established our expert in the inlet with a small building and cleared the area around the site including the water area in the inlet near the building. Our guru in the oyster experiment super-vised all this activity and bought oysters of his choice from local merchants. He implanted the oysters with the grain of sand, which again our man had personally found. He announced he had implanted the sand in about 1000 oysters and placed them in the salt water in "pens." He was very secretive about what he was doing which was fine as long as his secretive actions paid off. He explained that the oyster needed two years to do their thing. He advised that the first pearls might not be of commercial grade but in time he believe could pro-vide pearls that would be salable. I realized based upon what I had been told in Japan that this was not an over-night miracle but a lengthy project time wise. One had to be patient to achieve success. He brought his wife into the project, which I approved, and he hired several men from our work force to learn the trade. I of course told Dr. Lee what I done and what I had agreed to with this gent, and Dr. Lee didn't think I was crazy but just shook his head. He said he had not been surprised at the successes that we had achieved and prayed that our oyster caper might also pay off. Time would tell. I had ten folks on my payroll who worked very little, but the payoff I was told would return our investment in spades. We just had to wait a few years while our oysters did their thing. I asked our guy if there was any profit in developing a clam farm to sell the product. He liked the idea and thought he could handle that chore with his team and turn a profit much quicker than the pearl project. He established a clam farm and within six months he was selling clams on the market with a pretty good return. Clams seemed to like us better than oysters! I steamed a lot of clams the next few years with my fingers crossed hoping for the oysters to make pearls. We had over a thousand oysters in our oyster pens. It was fun to go over to the oyster pens and do a little fertility dance. Probably the wrong kind of dance, but I wanted our pearl program to work! Our pearl guy, whose name by the way was Sui, came to me one day and said that if we got a good quality bunch of pearls they should be made into jewelry for the market. Surprisingly, he said his wife made jewelry in Japan and would be available if I wanted to use her. I asked to see any samples that she had created and he showed me several and I got them got them okayed by Abby! I hired her for when the first successful batch of oysters produced.

It happened! The magic two-year day arrived, and Sui started to open a small batch of our implanted oysters. Out of the first fifty he opened, each one had a pearl, but most were gnarly and of no use for jewelry even after polishing; however, out of the fifty there were about ten that had made a very nice and let me call it—beautiful pearl. After Sui polished them, they were beautiful and of sufficient quality to be made into attractive jewelry. So out of fifty we got ten, that's a return of 20% for our investment. Needless to say we put 5,000 more implanted oysters into out oyster pens and waited another two years. We set aside about 100 of the original batch and let them sit for another year. We got a 50% return of good pearls from that batch so we were learning, but slowly! The market was there on our finished jewelry as our Asian brethren loved pearl jewelry. Me too!

# Chapter 11

# Rubber and War Room

Lee Industries had started out with its first serious moneymaking production by planting hundreds of rubber trees on its property. It had become a money maker and had provided a good living for Dr. Lee's father and family. The primary goal for the natural rubber was as the prime product in the development of tires. With the demand for tire and other rubber products for military use during the war, most rubber producing countries in Southeast Asia were in Japan's hands as Japan had no capability for producing rubber and was one of the prime reasons for their taking over Southeast Asia in 1941.

"Rubber has unique material properties that allow it to be strong, durable, flexible, abrasion resistant and extremely waterproof. Natural rubber is derived from the latex from rubber trees. Tapping the bark of these trees allows the latex (sticky, milky colloid) to be drawn off by making incisions in the bark and collecting the fluid in vessels. The latex then is refined into rubber ready for commercial processing" (*This is a quote from Lake Erie Rubber and Manufacturing*). When WWII ended and the rubber industry in Southeast Asia was returned to the rightful owners, there was a boom for rubber products as the many countries were rebuilding after the destruction of the war. The U.S., though not destroyed during the war, flourished and grew, and the demand for rubber was in competition with Europe and Asia as the many countries were rebuilding following the devastation of the war. Rubber was in great demand during this booming rebuilding process. Lee Industries was in the most profitable position than it had been in years. Lee's rubber plantations were working at full speed by the occupying Japanese so when the Japanese were driven from Southeast Asia after the war, the rubber plantations continued to boom under their rightful owners supplying the rebuilders throughout the world. Lee Industries cleared the land and planted more rubber trees to take advantage of the need for rubber. This boom lasted for about ten to fifteen years, and the demand for rubber started to diminish in the 1960s. The rubber needs switched from rebuilding needs to automobile and farm equipment needs again with a heavy need for rubber. Lee's had boomed during the years after the war with the demand for rubber the world over and continued as the automobile demand continued to grow. This was about the time Janssen came on the scene and opened up other markets for Lee. Janssen had recognized that Lee's fortune relied chiefly on rubber and tin from the mines, but he envisioned that their land that was laying fallow could be revised to produce more income and profit. The oil and natural gas simply fell into his lap and tuned out pretty simple to make large profits for Lee. A new market for the rubber popped up from an unlikely source as Jeff our ship builder had received a very large government contract for additional harbor and inshore boats and small ships. Rubber was required in multiple ways for these numerous boats. The need was not for sheets of rubber but for bulk rubber manufactured into many small parts for numerous needs. Jeff had locally the capability of fashioning the manufacturing of the many small rubber parts but needed our bulk rubber to utilize the manufacturing of rubber parts.

We had found a readily available and reliable market for our rubber in Jeff, which provided a steady income from our rubber sales to him. Our ships had been carefully designed to carry fuel, both bulk oil and LNG. We ordered two more ships from Jeff that were strictly bulk carriers of rubber, tin, frozen meat, and an occasional pearl!

This gave us a fleet of twenty ships that were hard working and constantly underway delivering our products. We had a busy staff keeping track of our ships and schedules. We had created a "war room" in our offices that were manned 24/7 by a crew that I had trained by hit and miss to control our fleet. You can't make money from a ship sitting in some port alongside a pier; they must be kept moving with a full cargo for a foreign port or moving empty under ballast returning to home port to reload. Interspersed with these activities, maintenance time hopefully scheduled must be woven into the ship's schedule. Don't forget the crew! Most of our ships' crews consisted of about sixteen men with a captain down to the lowest able seaman. If we were doing our scheduling job, rarely did we have a ship waiting to unload or load in home port or in foreign ports. We kept our pier busy and fully manned to service our ships. We did very little maintenance aboard our ships but at scheduled times ashore. We used the Blue and Gold crew concept that our U.S. submarines use. The Blue Crew would be aboard for six months and then ashore for six months while the Gold Crew took over. One can see why we needed the "war room" to direct the scheduling of our busy ships and crews. Sounds complicated but I loved it and spent a lot of my time in the war room.

My life as a younger man, like all folks, was a history of ups and downs. Whenever I was riding high, I used to say to myself, watch out, don't get too high or a fall may be coming!

# Chapter 12

# The Explosion

A fall indeed! We had an LNG ship in port taking on LNG when we had a major explosion at the fueling station that put a major crimp in our shipping and most of our other businesses for six months while we recovered. We almost lost the ship, but rapid response from our own firefighting crews and the port's alert firefighters were able to contain the fires caused by the explosion. The explosion put the ship into repair for months and tore up (destroyed) 150 feet of our pier including most of our refueling rigs on both sides of the pier. We were very lucky as the only loss of life were from our folks working on the pier on that one ship. We lost four men killed outright and eight others who were hospitalized but all recovered. Our total damage from the explosion including pier and ship totaled $1.5 million dollars. Our insurance took care of most of the damage and compensation for our dead and injured. It of course set back Lee Industries losses in revenue of close to six months while we worked very hard to put our pier and equipment back into working order.

An investigation by our people and the Singapore port authorities showed that a worker from our loading crew had not fully seated the probe into the ship's receiver and LNG leaked during the transfer of fuel. Of course nearby an idiot lit up his cigarette and BOOM! went the explosion. We made some changes in safety supervision whenever we fueled one of our ships. Unfortunately, we did not have a ship alongside the damaged pier for four months. Much of our ship traffic came to a halt as we backed up our ships in other ports while we repaired our pier and equipment. Our losses were in the millions of dollars, while we worked feverishly to get back into running our company. The families of the killed were compensated generously as were the injured. Lee Industries had never been considered a company that didn't stand by for it employees and the company fully confirmed that reputation for the dead and injured. I had been working in the war room in our office building when the explosion occurred and it blew out most windows on our side of the building. There were a few cuts and bruised folks but nothing too serious that our own medical staff couldn't handle.

Dr. Lee flew to Singapore as soon as he heard the news. His presence was most valuable working with the insurance companies and the compensation for the dead and injured. Abby and I put him up as he no longer had a home in Singapore.

His first reaction when we got together was a degree of anger as he suggested perhaps that we (me) had been moving too fast and the explosion occurred perhaps from a lack of supervision in our overall safety program. It was a surprise, as his opinion of me had always been of appreciation for what he had seen and what I had accomplished with his approval. It was difficult to argue with him as he was right; I had been moving the company pretty fast, but my thoughts were that this magnificent piece of land would still be planted with rubber trees and would not have provided so many people with wealth without my ideas. He cooled down as soon as he was with Abby, as always. He did apologize to me a short time later as he said he realized what I had done had not only made him wealthy but provided work for many hundreds of Singaporeans over the years. As a peace offering, I presented him with a magnificent set of a tie clasp and cuff links decorated with our cultured pearls. He liked them!

We set up a memorial on the pier with the names of those killed and those injured. There were a lot of questions about the man who failed to set the probe into the receiver and even more questions regarding the gent who lit his cigarette against all company rules. Both these gents were killed in the explosion, but we put their names on the memorial anyway, and Dr. Lee insisted that the families of both receive compensation for giving their lives to the company. The very large drawdown of revenue put emphasis heavily on the rubber, tin, meat, and sugar production. Even my pet project producing pearls got into the act, and it was as though our oysters were listening as the percentage of good pearls increased. The company was hit hard by the resultant drawdown of fuel sales as that had been our biggest moneymaker and the source of buying our fleet of ships. Our oil and natural gas continued filling up our storage tanks but simply laid dormant as we could not deliver any to our customers. We received a glimmer of hope as a sister exporter rented pier space to us to move our non-fuel products. Our pier that had all the whistles and bells for handing and pumping fuel to our ships was simply busted! We didn't simply sit on our hands while our pier was being repaired. Jock convinced me that this was the time to dig several more wells. He said he wanted lots of fuel available a soon as we could put our ships to work. Believe it or not we even ordered an additional LNG ship for delivery when this stoppage of our fuel delivery ended. I thought the boss might drop dead when I told him we were ordering another ship while our revenues were so low. He came around though as it was a good business decision.

Understandably, a lot of our workers, particularly those involved with fuel, were not fully employed. Due to our hiatus, we refused to lay any workers off at Dr. Lee's insistence, so found work for many of our fuel gangs in other areas of our company. Decisions such as this by Dr. Lee created an excellent workers' attitude and we were advised that our company was considered by many in Singapore as an excellent place to work. Our salaries were among the highest and the benefits many. When the unions tried to unionize Lee Industries, the workers themselves shunned them!

# Chapter 13

## Abby's Clinic

While we were trying to patch up our pier in Singapore, Abby was doing great things with her clinic. She had expanded her hospital from an original 25-bed hospital to one that could accommodate 100 patients. Many of her patients were kids who did not need hospitalization but only out-patience care. The beds were primarily for recovery for surgical patients. The wealthy patients mostly had private rooms for which they paid dearly as that was the procedure that Abby used to finance her pro bono work. Any poor kid in Singapore with a hair lip had better hide or Abby will get you. Abby was a natural working with kids and we had a library full of pictures of her holding her recovered children. As a means of paying our respects to Dr. Lee for many past favors and as her original benefactor, she named her original clinic The Andrew Lee Children's Hospital. I mentioned earlier that when Dr. Lee gave A by and me 25% of ownership in Lee Industries, her eyes had lit up and she had found a place to put her newly found wealth into her clinic. I had agreed, as it became an every evening occurrence to hear Abby tell me the good things she was doing with our money.

# Chapter 14

## Twins (Again) and Richard

M left off my discussion of my twins when Abby and I got them settled in Stanford to do their residency in pediatrics with child surgery as part of the training. It was a two-year commitment but it was what the girls wanted. Both Laurie and Lisa finished with little difference between their grades as both were touted by their instructors, doctors, and nurses as outstanding young doctors who both were offered positions at the Stanford Hospital as Abby had been when she finished her training there. Abby, Richard, and the old man all flew to California for the twins' graduation from their training. It wasn't a formal graduation ceremony. We made a quick trip to Rhode Island to touch base with my mom and dad so the proud grandparents could rave about their grandkids and try to spoil them. Laurie and Lisa still were adamant that they would join their mom's clinic as soon as we arrived back home. Abby was thoroughly pleased that the girls wanted to join her staff. I invited my folks to please come visit us in Singapore and I offered to pay for their flights round trip. They accepted and said to expect them within the next six months. We didn't do any more visiting in the U.S. as I was anxious to get back home and try to sort out the many details in putting our company back together after the explosion.

Richard had finished medical school and now as a full-fledged doctor had wonderful discussions with his sisters and their mom about medical details that were way over my head, but it was fun to hear the four of them discussing and arguing over high points of medicine. Richard had shown little interest in leaving Singapore for his residency and had been accepted in Singapore at the hospital to pursue his residency in orthopedics focusing on children as had his mom and sisters. Abby had told him that if he so desired she would set him up with his own wing of her clinic devoted to working with kids in orthopedics. I groaned as I could see again part of our newfound wealth with the ownership of 25% of Lee Industries continue going into Abby's clinic (hospital)! I am exaggerating as I fully supported Abby's work and now my kids. We had taken a pretty big hit on our income as a result of the explosion but could see the light at the end of the tunnel with our pier repair.

I hadn't been spending much time on our boat as I directed most of my time and effort to the repair of our pier. You'll remember we had four stations on our pier where we could work (load) four ships at a time. This was a bit overkill but occasionally we would be forced to handle four ships in spite of our planning and scheduling of ship arrival and departures.

With four ships alongside, it spread our loading crews pretty thin and it always worried me about safety after our recent calamity. As the repair of our four stations proceeded and our ship handling started to get back to a busy but normal pace, I found that I had more time to work on my golf game.

# Chapter 15

# Seafood

In the foursome I occasionally played with, there was a salty old guy who used to rave about all the crabs and shrimp he would gather and eat and share with his friends including my family. I once asked him if I could join him on one of his seafood trips to watch and learn how he did the trapping of these succulent critters. He did, and I carefully noted each had their own seasons, but the seasons were pretty long as these were tropical waters and there was little fishing to deplete the supply. He baited his traps with old spoiled fish and poultry. That was on his crab traps. He had about ten wire made traps stacked on his deck for crab and I'm told a similar number for shrimp. He said he baited his shrimp traps with old spoiled meat. Baiting was a tad smelly, but it worked.

It was fun to watch him lay his traps in a string each with his colored buoy for identification. After laying his traps, he would haul off about a half-mile and break out the beer and smokes and sit for a couple of hours while the crabs did their thing. He told me he followed the same procedure for shrimp but the traps were of a different design to allow the smaller shrimp to crawl into the traps to get at the bait. The crabs were large mostly two to three pounds, and the shrimp quite big but with a large head that was disposed of leaving a good sized body with the meat.

Always looking for a way to make a buck I bought, on my own, ten each of the crab and shrimp traps. I approached my pearl man, Sui, and invited him to go crabbing with me with a couple of his key folks. They enjoyed the change of pace from waiting for the oysters to do their thing. I think they mostly enjoyed the two-hour break for beer and smokes while the critters took the bait. I asked Sui if he and his pearl crew might like to do this trapping on their own and for a profit. I told him I would buy him a boat fully equipped for trapping and it just needed men to work the process. He became very excited and said, "Yes! I would like to do that!" It didn't take long for me to find a used boat for sale, buy the traps, help Sui train his crews, and we were in the crab and shrimp business. We built a small pier on the inlet where Sui had his oyster pens but far enough away to not bother the oysters. The market for crab and shrimp was readily available in Singapore, and though it did not make us rich, it did bring in a steady income. It was pleasant for Sui and his crew to be busy while waiting for their pearls! In those days we could fish in the Straits of Malacca without even a license and with very little competition. Sui and his folks were happy to get involved as I think waiting for the oysters to do their thing was boring. I should mention that our seafood project caught on with the local populace and our business grew to five boats and employed 100 people.

# Chapter 16

# Finished

We finally got our pier put back together, and the new wells that Jock had dug while the pier was under repair provided much fuel that needed to be move to our Japanese customers. Within about four months following the repair efforts, we were back in business with the profits flowing into our coffers. Dr. Lee had returned to Bali, and Abby and I made at least a one-week long trip there to bring him up to speed and renew our old friendship. He of course as always was mostly interested in Abby and the progress of our kids. We had made him a very wealthy man and he was perhaps the most generous man in Southeast Asia in his donations to help many causes to make life better for the inhabitants of the countries of Southeast Asia. He was starting to show his age and was slowing down in all of his activities but still was the very wise and considerate gentleman that had offered me the job as his assistant all those many years earlier. Thanks, Dr. Lee.

**The End**